They approached the cliff shelf. Now a steeper slope was in front of them, and Bruce slipped on some loose shale as it skidded out from under him. "It's eroded and crumbling here, maybe we should—"

"Seems safe enough, if we're canny. Dinna' go directly down. There's the path that way. It's a bit rough, but it's been used recently and no' that long since." They proceeded cautiously and in silence for another fifty yards or so. Then suddenly Bruce heard his name being called by a familiar voice. Jeremy?

"Reverend Bruce, I'm over here!"

Moving quickly in the direction of the sound, the two men failed to notice the others until they were surrounded. A bunch of the roughest, toughest characters Bruce had seen anywhere since his curate days in the Glasgow slums, "the gang!" His heart sank as the ringleader stepped forward.

"Whit did ye have to come pokin' aboot for, reverend? We're goin' to have to kill ye noo an' yer faither here as weel!"

Bruce MacAlister, a devoted man of God, had first lost his beloved wife and then his small Scottish kirk. Was he now to lose his own life as he sought to save a young waif?

My Heart's in the Highlands

MOLLY GLASS

Power Books

Fleming H. Revell
Old Tappan, New Jersey

Scripture quotations in this volume are based on the King James Version of the Bible.

Library of Congress Cataloging-in-Publication Data

Glass, Molly.
  My heart's in the Highlands / Molly Glass.
    p.   cm.
  ISBN 0-8007-5289-9
  I. Title.
PS3557.L345M9 1989
813'.54—dc19

88-30197
CIP

Copyright © 1989 by Molly Glass
Published by the Fleming H. Revell Company
Old Tappan, New Jersey 07675
Printed in the United States of America

My Heart's in the Highlands

—◦⊰{ 1 }⊱◦—

Breakfast in the manse kitchen in the parish of Inverechny, on the Isle of Skye, began on that glorious April morning in the year of our Lord 1880, in exactly the same way as it had every morning for the past two years.

Hamish Cormack had risen early to get things ready. First he started by stirring up the smooth porridge made from oatmeal that had simmered all night long in the thick iron pot, where it hung suspended over a shining black grate. Cream, fresh that morning from the cows on the Gould farm, would smother the hearty cereal. Hamish hummed the tune Jean MacAlister had taught him, which she told him was called "Stracathro," as he cleared away the empty bowls and placed the eggs for Bruce in a smaller pan of boiling water. Turning the hourglass so that they would not go longer than exactly the two minutes, he quickly took up a slice of bread and stuck it on the toasting fork, to be lightly browned as Mistress Jean liked it. One small brown egg for Mary Jean and all would be ready. A half-dozen rashers of bacon sizzled to a crisp alongside a plateful of scrambled eggs for himself. As head cook and bottle washer for the minister's household he could have all the rashers he wanted to place in the immense frying pan. Wee Mary Jean liked to eat her egg without help, using her own bone spoon, and if more yolk reached her white bib than her mouth, it didn't matter a bit to her three admirers.

For the men, the lot would be washed down with quarts of strong, black tea. Sometimes Jean would enjoy a cup of the special coffee brew her granny would send her, but she had used up the last of it a week ago.

Reverend Bruce MacAlister cast a pleased, possessive smile over the occupants of his table just as his wife turned from wiping Mary Jean's egg-smeared face. Their eyes met, and she blushed deeply, almost dazzled by the blueness of her husband's gaze of benign love. She shook her head warningly, but Hamish caught the look. He jumped up.

"Mustna' sit here a' day. Ah've the dishes to do and the spring cleanin' to start on."

Jean glanced his way. "Never mind the dishes this nice morning, Hamish, and you can start the cleaning tomorrow. Take Mary Jean to see the lambs at the Gould's and bring back an extra gill of cream. I've a notion to make some rice pudding with raisins for supper."

"I will that, but first I'll take doon the curtains for a soak and then I'll wash them later on. You're not to touch them, mind!"

Jean laughed. "Never fear, Hamish. If I dust the cabinet with Granny's ornaments, I'll be doing well for today."

Bruce spoke up then. "The cabinet can wait. I'll finish off my sermon for Sunday. Then I'll be back for an hour to help you with the china."

"Oh, Bruce, the china is an easy job I can do sitting down. It's about time I started doing a bit more all together. Remember what Mistress Johnstone said last week when she called for tea and saw Hamish out the back beating the carpet."

"When I'm ready to take my orders from the villagers, I'll be up and away across the watter. We'll not risk your health for any village woman and her wagging tongue." Hamish had finished removing the curtains from the kitchen window before dragging the large wooden washtub to the middle of the floor. He poured a pannikin of hot water from the tank in the range.

"Hear, hear!" He agreed heartily with Bruce regarding Mistress Johnstone but then Hamish agreed with him about most things. Mary's voice chimed from her special chair, where she was trying to untie the straps. Her uncle had built it for her, making it childproof so that she couldn't get out of it by herself.

"Uncle Hamie, Mary wants to see the lambs." Mary had never used baby talk, and Bruce beamed at his daughter. What a wonder she was. He waved at Hamish.

"Go then, Hamish. I'll help Jean take the hooks off the curtains before I go to the kirk to study. It'll be an easy enough matter to douse them in the soapy water."

Half an hour later Jean sat alone in her kitchen. This was the coziest room in the house, and the furniture had been chosen and placed for her convenience, although Hamish and Bruce between them did all the work. From a hassock, placed strategically in front of the wooden washtub, she idly moved the plunger back and forth in the sudsy foam. Patterns in the foam set her mind soaring with ideas, and she wished she had asked one of the men to fetch her notebook from the bedroom upstairs. *Upstairs* really was too grand a term for the six narrow steps leading to their bedroom, but they marked an insurmountable barrier for her. The men in the family treated her like one of those fine porcelain ornaments in the parlor cabinet that she had intended to dust this morning. Maybe the men didn't care about what Mistress Johnstone and the other neighbors might say but Jean always cringed at the scorn registered on the lady's face when she glanced round the manse. Idyllic as Jean Irvine MacAlister's life seemed, there were times, like today, when she felt smothered by the loving attentions heaped upon her. Surely she had taken a long time to recover from Mary's birth. She shuddered, remembering the warnings from Dr. Lockhart, echoed strongly by Bruce's friend Dr. Peter Blair. Even the village nurse still lectured her about her weakened condition. But now she felt well enough and was gaining strength with every passing day.

"I'm going to start making wee changes in the pattern!" She spoke the words to Bella MacRae's cat from next door. Tippy was making her morning call and would expect the usual saucer of cream set out for her by Hamish, with Mary Jean's messy help, but today they had left without doing it.

Absently thinking of her notebook, lying on the bedside table, since she had been making entries last night after Bruce had fallen asleep, she moved slowly to the cupboard set in the window, where they kept the cream jug. It was empty! The cat gave her a look of disgust, and she found herself apologizing to it.

"Sorry, Tippy, but I'm feeling frustrated myself this morning. I want to do so much and can do so little. We'll both just have to be patient until they come back from the farm." She smiled as the cat marched past her with its tail pointing straight up in the air.

"You'll be back." Her thoughts returned to the earlier track of finding a way to break the comfortable monotony of her day.

All Jean's life she had been waited upon. During her early years in India, where her father, Colonel Cameron Irvine of the Queen's Own Regiment had been stationed in the Punjab, there had been servants to anticipate her every need. Furloughs spent at Granny's, in Strathcona House, had not been much better. She'd had fewer servants in Glasgow, but faithful Betsy Degg would only allow Miss Jean, as she still called her, to help with what she considered the ladylike tasks of setting the table when Granny had paying guests.

Her memories stopped there to linger for a while as she recalled her first meeting with Bruce MacAlister. He had been one of Granny's boarders, and she laughed aloud, remembering the days of their strange courtship. He teased her often about she being the hunter and he the helpless prey, but she knew it was true. Why, they might not be married yet, if she had not taken the initiative there. Then there had been Peter Blair, Bruce's best friend. Dr. Peter Blair now, of course, and at present deeply involved with his practice in the Gorbals, a sad slum district of Glasgow. Bruce had spent his first summer as a curate in that same district. According to Granny's last letter, Peter's courtship of young Agatha Rose Gordon, Granny's friend's granddaughter, was sailing along more on the lines expected of respectable young ladies of this age and era. Jean laughed softly again. She was not a bit sorry to have missed that. Granny had also said the couple were having a bit of trouble agreeing on where Peter would practice after the marriage. The end results should be interesting. Maybe Lachlan the Postie would bring her a letter today, with the latest news. He should be here soon.

For many months after Mary's birth Jean had not been allowed to take so much as one step on her own, and she had never gone out of her room unless Bruce had been there to carry her. Gradually they had allowed her to walk a few steps at a time, until now she could cross the room without aid. Oh, how she prayed that God would heal her completely. There was so much she wanted to do. Scolding herself, she thought, *This mood must only be because I don't have my notebook and pencils.* The books she wanted to read were in the parlor. Well, she would just have to go and get one of them. This was as good a day as any to change the rules. Leaving the protection of the wall, where she had been leaning, she resolved to try to walk a bit faster and a bit farther this time.

It happened so fast that no one could ever get a clear picture of it. Tippy, still anticipating her saucer of cream, had padded silently back to the warm place in the sun. The unshaded windows made the patch larger than usual today. Intent on her own errand, Jean was not aware of the creature until her foot crunched on its tail and the animal screeched in protest as it leaped to escape. Jean's cry of horror echoed the cat's as she felt herself falling, falling, falling. The padded hassock made contact with her shinbone as she pitched forward and over it, but it was not enough to halt her momentum. Her head hit the table edge with a sharp crack, and she lay still.

Lachlan MacLachlan, no animal lover at the best of times, was delivering the post. He gave a startled yell when the cat streaked past him where he stood on the manse doorstep, waiting to hammer on the door with his fist as he always did to warn the mistress of the manse that he was coming in. Moments later he swung the door fully open, calling out as he strode across the kitchen floor, "Mistress MacAlister, you've a lot of letters the day. Two fae Glasgow and one fae Aribaig as well as one fae furreign pairts. I'll just leave them on the table. I—aah!" That was when he saw her. At first Jean's red hair almost hid the pool of blood seeping under it. Something was far wrong. Abandoning his precious bag, bearing the seal and insignia of Her Majesty's royal mail, Lachlan quickly knelt down beside the stricken woman. He lifted one limp hand.

"Dear God Almighty, but she's awa' this time!"

As an answer to Mistress Armstrong's pathetic plea of "What shall I do?" The Reverend Bruce MacAlister only paused long enough to indicate his wife's bureau before rushing headlong from the room.

"Her grandmother. Tell her to come!" His words echoed through the open door, and the understanding nurse gazed compassionately after his disappearing back. Assuring herself he would do nothing rash, she turned to the miserable jobs she had yet to face.

So she made up the telegram in her mind as she walked along the well-worn path to the postie's house. Her thoughts flew back to the last telegram she had sent for the minister. That time it had announced the good news of wee Mary Jean MacAlister's early arrival into the world. If young Mistress MacAlister had had to die, she, Victoria Armstrong, would have said it should have happened then and not this day.

She left the sad little message with Lachlan MacLachlan. He would start the awful news on its journey across the miles of wires strung on poles the length and breadth of the land, to arrive, she knew not how, at the abode of the old lady whose name she remembered from that other, happier occasion. Poor old soul. Slowly making her way back to the dreaded house of mourning, Mistress Armstrong stopped for a moment to gaze across the Lang Ford, so deceptively beautiful and peaceful on this lovely April morning. Her thoughts raced. The news would bring mourners from all the different places on the mainland from which she knew Mistress MacAlister's many letters had come and gone.

The minister had disappeared in the direction of the moor, and his terrible shout, "What for?" still echoed in Victoria's ears. Hamish Cormack, the reverend's reformed-renegade brother, had left earlier, taking two-year-old Mary MacAlister back to Elliott Gould's croft. Elliott had a special interest in the bairn, having been present at her birthing.

A dry sob escaped the midwife as she pondered that wild night two years ago, still talked of as "the night of the miracle," and all her medical training would have made her think that night should have held a triple tragedy. Instead Bruce MacAlister and his stepbrother, Hamish, had survived a night of exposure in the freezing waters of the Lang Ford, and Jean MacAlister had survived one of the worst hemorrhages she had ever seen in all her years as a midwife.

It should have happened to the mistress of the manse then. Immediately she admonished herself for the thought. Who was she to dictate to the Almighty? Victoria was not a praying woman; nevertheless she prayed now: "Dear God, let this message not kill the soul so closely knit with young Mistress MacAlister. Help me to ease my mind, too, Lord. I know there's nothing any of us could have done. Dr. Lockhart even said that if Jean MacAlister had lived after the fall she would have been completely helpless and paralyzed in the bargain. Hard as it seems, maybe it's a blessin'. . . ." She choked before going on with the simple prayer. "It canna be made a better o' now, so help us all no' to make it worse. Amen."

Beginning to walk faster she soon reached the door of the manse. Her man would be coming with the carpenter and all the dreaded paraphernalia to make the necessary wooden box.

Bella MacRae, Victoria's neighbor who helped her on these occasions, waited on the doorstep, and the two women began their grim task. They worked in silence for a while but finally Bella spoke up, "You sent the word then, Victoria?"

"I did that, Bella. Her poor old granny in Glasgow will learn it soon enough now. She and Mistress MacAlister were awful close and the terrible news I had to tell could not be softened."

Bella stopped working to gape at the nurse. Sometimes the big words came out to remind folk of her higher education than the rest of the villagers of Inverechny, but this did not seem to be the reason today. Could Victoria be crying? She risked another comment: "I'm that glad Dr. Lockhart decided no autopsy would be necessary. Thon's a—"

But this was too much for the professional woman's dignity: "That's no' our business, Bella. Hand me that gown." Put sharply in her place, Bella subsided.

Meanwhile, in a mansion house in George Street, Glasgow, the interruption to the quiet little dinner party caused a distinct feeling of déjà-vu to sweep over Amelia Godfrey as she heard the words, "Go to her!" But without hesitation she stepped up to the older lady and took a position behind her.

Purely by instinct, George Bennett had directed his friend to go to Mistress Beulah MacIntyre moments after the maid, Betsy, had entered the drawing room, bearing a tray on which lay a sinister yellow envelope. A sense of unidentified fear pervaded the room as he leaned over to pick up the telegram. Betsy was shaking so hard she nearly dropped the tray.

His hostess asserted herself. "For goodness sake, what is it, Betsy, and why are we all so stricken? Will someone please explain?" George proffered the envelope, but Beulah, for all her brave talk, promptly fainted at the sight of it.

Ripping the message open George read aloud:

"Jean is dead! Come. MacAlister."

Bruce MacAlister made his blind progress up to the moors to mourn alone, striding along the well-beaten path with no true purpose except his desire for escape—escape back to that time before the moment of revelation, before the postman had cried his name and spilled out the dreadful, unbelievable news that his beloved Jean had left him forever. Reaching the fork in the path, he veered off toward the uphill climb, oblivious to the glory of the scene before him or that the hour was not yet noon. A gull screamed overhead, and Bruce's answering scream was longer and more bitter than the bird's. Full of rage and frustration and every other emotion experienced by men at such a time, he shook a tightly clenched fist heavenward while crying out to God the age-old lament: "Why? Why my Jean, when it should have been me? It's all so meaningless. If she was too good for me, why was I allowed to have her for such a short while? Was it just to torment me? Not nearly long enough to show her how much I did love her. I didn't deserve her, but oh, how I need her—and Mary. What am I to do with Mary?" Throwing himself face down on the spongy, moss-covered peat, he lay prostrate for a time. Then the screaming began afresh. "I'll not work for You. I'll not be a minister for You. I'll not preach another sermon for You. Sorry words they would be, when I have no answers or comfort to offer! Having none for myself after this—this . . . !" Smashing with his fists, he beat on the ground relentlessly, caring nothing about his own bleeding and torn flesh. Overcome at last, he sobbed out his failure, and the echo of his cry, "I'll not. I'll not!" was taken up by the uncaring gulls swooping and circling in the sky above his head. Finally the oblivion he sought washed over him, and he slept like one dead.

2

Much more than stepbrotherhood linked Hamish Cormack and Bruce MacAlister. Their shared night of miracles bound them with ties much closer than earthly or brotherly love. Since that time it had been enough for Hamish to know that his life was no longer his own. He now belonged to Bruce and, through Bruce, to Bruce's Lord, Jesus. Waking from the ordeal of that never-to-be-forgotten night, Hamish had not wasted a moment in tracking Bruce from the humble beachcomber's hut to the manse in Inverechny. From then on he had become a shadow to Bruce, to his wife, Jean, and to wee Mary Jean as well.

Guessing where the "meenister," as the villagers called his stepbrother, would be on this terrible day of bereavement, Hamish left Mary Jean with Elliott Gould and his cozy wife while he sought Bruce out. As he loped along the heather path he, too, questioned himself cruelly on what he might have done to avoid the morning's tragedy.

Finding Bruce lying facedown on the heather, where his blood-spattered hands and head had smashed on the ground, Hamish cried out in anguish, "Am I too late?" Quickly assuring himself that Bruce was very much alive, he settled down for a time of waiting.

While Bruce slept, totally oblivious, Hamish sat on the

heather beside him and watched. His mind, weary of trying to think of how this terrible accident could have been avoided, veered now to the much talked of night two years ago. In those days he knew that, not only the villagers of Inverechny scorned him completely, but most of the folks on the other islands hereabouts, as well as on the mainland, despised him. He hadn't cared much then, and now, knowing he was a changed being, he didn't worry about it either.

Lachlan MacLachlan, the postmaster, who could never resist being first with the news, telling it to whoever would listen, had related his version of the night's doings to Hamish, filling in the gaps in the ex-ferryman's memory: how the young minister's wife had nearly died in childbed; how the minister himself, out answering a call, had near drowned.

Hamish had listened without saying much at first, then, "You say this Josiah Burns saw us comin' oot the watter?"

"Saw you, man, he says you were walkin' on the watter!" As this was what Hamish himself believed he did not argue the point. Josiah Burns was not known for his honest doings but then again, no one could have spent more than an hour or two in that freezing water in the middle of a twister and survived without other than human aid.

A thrill ran through Hamish, and he had ventured another question at the all-knowing Lachlan, "Did you ken the reverend is my brother?"

"Aye, we ken now. The meenister called you Hamish." The two men eyed each other; then Lachlan asked his own question. "*Hamish*, is it? We thought you were *Hector Dermott* when you worked for the ferryman." At that Hamish had turned and walked away.

A strangled sound brought his mind to the present horror. Bruce was coming out of his dwam. The man lying on the ground stirred and groaned. Hamish sighed deeply. The worst would come with the wakening.

3

The sound of Peter's swearing echoed through the summerhouse, bounced off the latticed walls, and ended in a spate of untenable questions for George Bennett, "Where is your God now, Mr. Pulpit Bennett? Where is the MacAlister's God now? Eh? Oh, 'tis glad I am that I cling not to such empty hopes. Why that poor lass? What happened and why the now? Just when we thought she was over the worst. Och, what's the use?" Peter turned away from George, pounding his clenched fist into his other hand.

"I'm asking questions myself, Peter, lad. But my friend Amelia has asked me one, and I can only repeat it to you. 'What are our options?' Surely in times like this the hope does seem empty. However, when you think on it, there is no such thing as empty hope. Ye either have it, or ye don't have it. Put that way, I prefer to have it. We, that is, Amelia and I, know that whatever way it happened, Jean slipped directly into the full presence of the Lord Jesus. It will take Bruce MacAlister, and even Beulah MacIntyre, a while longer to remember that, but remember it they will." For fully a minute their eyes locked. George's held the gentle gaze of love and a yearning to be understood, Peter's held a glare of near hatred. Peter lowered his gaze first.

Patting his arm, George said, "Sorry to be the bearer of such ill tidings, but someone had to tell you, Peter. Well, I must be

18

off now." Leaving him alone in the summerhouse, Agatha Rose
having fled at Peter's angry and blasphemous shouts, George
glanced back over his shoulder. "Will you go to your friend?"

"I'll go! But I don't know what I'll say or if it will do any
good."

"You'll do good, never doubt that. I'll away, then." Peter sat
down on the hard bench where so recently he and Agatha had
been laughing like a pair of foolish children in what seemed
another life. He kept pounding the one fist into the other as the
full impact of the terrible news sank in. Should he go? All the
holies would be there, and he didn't know if he could stomach
that. He groaned inside, sensing somehow that Bruce would
need him, if only to scold him back to his senses, because he,
Peter Blair, the practical physician, knew there would be a
period of near oblivion before sharp reality returned in earnest.

"I'll go." He spoke aloud to the uncaring benches once again,
"Of course I'll go, and I'll not need to get the cost of the fare
from my father, either. I have thon tickets to Oban I bought on
the occasion of the Highlandman's wedding. I hope they're still
valid." A sob caught in his throat as he recalled buying the
tickets. Indeed he must go, because strong as Bruce MacAlister
thought he was, he would need the understanding of his
thick-skinned doctor friend.

That first *why* screamed out by Bruce to God and carried on
the wind to be echoed by the unheeding gulls, also echoed in
varying degrees to those who shared in the agony of his
desolation. Peter Blair had stormed in the first stab of grief and
shouted his anger at the news bringer, not because the man
brought the news but because, in that moment, George Bennett
represented God to Peter. The young doctor, strangely and
paradoxically, for someone not fully persuaded that God ex-
isted, still blamed God for the tragedy.

In Strathcona House the *why* echoed softly but with the same
desolation from the heart of Beulah MacIntyre. She received no
immediate answer either, so except for that first wavering

moment, Jean's grandmother responded with her inborn stoicism. Some of those about her saw through to the deeper hurt but wisely refrained from useless comment. Their own *whys* remained unanswered. Beulah breathed hers into heartfelt prayer, ending it with: ". . . Nevertheless not my will but Thy will, O God. Your ways are past our finding out."

Agatha Rose Gordon, her face red and swollen with weeping, showed her feelings more openly. Although she had hardly known the dead Jean MacAlister, her pain was no less real and no less terrible. All her own short life, Agatha's thoughts and aims had been geared toward the domestic life, sprinkled with the tingling hopes and fears only read about in the romantic stories she so avidly devoured. Now suddenly her easy life had been invaded by something real and terrifying. Never wavering from her plan to marry Peter Blair someday, she now placed that decision aside for the time being. Why, if Jean Irvine hadn't been in such a hurry to get married, she could still be alive. With thoughts of Jean invading her mind, Agatha burst into a fresh outbreak of tears and sobs.

"Och, Miss Agatha if you dinna stop yer greetin', yer face'll stay swollen up, and you'll not be so bonny." The sobbing ceased abruptly, and Agatha turned her anguished eyes toward the cook, who had entered the drawing room quietly, after having soothed a hysterical Betsy.

Agatha choked back a final sob as she asked, "Why do things like this have to happen, Cook? Jean's so young yet. Not much older than me."

"Only the Guid Lord Hissel' knows, miss. Come awa' wi' me to the kitchen, and I'll get ye some o' thon ice left from the puddin's. Ye'll comb yer hair and dab on a bit powder to be mair like yersel'. The mistress is restin' at last. Dr. Peter gave her a potion before he went awa'." Agatha sighed with relief. At least Peter wouldn't be seeing her in this mess. Perhaps, too, she could forget having heard him mouthing those terrible curses. Meekly she followed Cook MacLaren to the kitchen for the ice water.

Sharing the loss and feeling the hurt of it, from the extremity of Beulah's grief to the fringe of unhappiness invading young Agatha's hitherto uncomplicated life, the small group in Glasgow's Central Station's first-class waiting room sat in silence. All the words possible had been said, and the emotions within them could not yet be voiced. Benny Stout, the porter whom George Bennett had commissioned to make sure the MacIntyre party had every possible comfort and assistance, was ready to use his wealth of experience in any way he could.

Beulah, dressed in deep-black velvet and looking very regal indeed, with Agatha Rose close by her side, pressed a frail hand tightly into Peter's as he helped her step down from the carriage, betraying to the sensitive doctor her tremulous weakness.

Unable to keep still, after leading Jean's granny to a seat, Peter paced the carpet. The women's eyes followed his every move. The younger, when she caught his glance, lowered her lashes demurely. Peter, not totally unaware of Aggie's scrutiny, nevertheless let his mind race ahead to what inevitably awaited them at the end of the journey. He halted his agitated pacing to burst out: "Blasted train! How much longer will we have to wait here?"

This was Benny's territory, and he answered, "I'll just go and look at the board again. It should be posted by now."

"Wait!" Beulah's voice broke in, and every eye veered in her direction. "We will take her back to Glasgow for burial in the family vault! Will you see to the arrangements with the railway company for that, Benny, please?" Beulah's announcement told her listeners that she would now resume control, following a temporary lapse into weakness. Earlier she had asked Peter to take care of dispatching the necessary telegraphs to Aribaig and to the Punjab, while Cook MacLaren and Betsy had been instructed to direct the shrouding of Strathcona House in the customary black draperies and hangings. Weeping afresh, the servants had complied, knowing not how else to express their deep grief.

At these orders now Benny looked to the doctor for confirmation.

Peter exploded again: "Begging your pardon, Mistress Mac, but you don't know what you're saying. Indeed your suggestion is totally inadvisable. By now the—" Belatedly catching a warning signal wildly flashing at him from Agatha, he stopped in mid-sentence. What he had almost said about a body decomposing and the two and a half days already passed blessedly remained unspoken. Benny left quickly, and silence reigned again; but soon the door leading onto the platform opened, and he reentered, closing it firmly behind him.

"Twenty minutes and it will be leaving. I have that from the station master himself. I've brought the barrow here for the cases, and I'll load them up now. Have no worries about anything on that score. It's all right, Dr. Blair. I can manage. It's my job, mind, so if you'll just escort the ladies to platform nine. Ye have the tickets?" As Peter nodded Benny busied himself with the various cases, one on his shoulder, one under the other arm, and one in each hand. Peter glanced toward Aggie, who giggled uncontrollably. The man *did* look funny. Beulah and Peter exchanged fleeting smiles just as the porter announced that their train could now be boarded.

The journey proved uneventful, the travelers being too exhausted physically and emotionally to hold much conversation. Upon arrival at the station they were met by Bruce's mother and grandfather, intent on the same errand. Not waiting for the ferry, Peter hired a private boat to convey them all to the tiny landing at Inverechny.

In the village all business had been suspended, and a pall hung over the place. Not a soul ventured out on the street, but the visitors were aware of eyes watching from the draped windows of the scattered cottages.

Inside the manse the same awful gloom waited, and Agatha

was ready to cry again, but she remembered the warnings about her face just in time. Besides, Peter was somewhere about, although he had paid her scant attention since the news arrived. She subsided into a corner of the room and watched the others.

Beulah MacIntyre and Bruce's mother, Elspeth Cormack, were in complete agreement at last. Jean would have rejoiced, had she lived to see this, although the circumstances and the reasons would have hurt her afresh. Elspeth had always blamed the old lady for encouraging her granddaughter and Bruce to marry far too early, in Elspeth's opinion, and although she had come to know and love Jean, she had never been reconciled to Beulah until now. Both were sure Mary Jean could not be left here, with Bruce in the state of mind he was in at present. To Beulah's suggestion of transporting Jean's body in a sealed coffin, to Glasgow, for burial, Elspeth made no comment. She would have felt the same, were it her own beloved son who lay there and not his dead wife. In common with many of the others here, Elspeth's thoughts flew back two years, to the happier occasion when there had been a gathering in this manse. What if Bruce and—God did have strange ways!—Hamish, too, had been swept out to sea in that twister the local people still described so vividly as the worst in living memory? This whole business was turning into a morbid nightmare, and the sooner they got away the better. Jean's body to Glasgow, if that was what her grandmother desired, and wee Mary, the lamb, who did not know and could not guess the turmoil going on about her, would come with them to Aribaig. Bruce's place was there, too, when he was ready to face life again.

"No! No! No!" The shouts rose to the beamed ceiling, rebounded, and hit the silence like trumpet blares. Bruce had been sitting morosely in his chair, oblivious to surroundings and people. When spoken to, he would merely nod vaguely in that person's direction. Even Peter was making no headway with him, having tried everything from friendly overtures to cursing insults. His friend would take no nourishment whatsoever, and no amount of coaxing or threats changed his expression. The arrangements for the funeral had not reached him until Beulah, trying to understand herself, yet wishing not to offend Bruce, had spoken of her plans to take Jean's body to Glasgow. Bruce's inertia had left him that instant.

Beulah had tried again, "But Bruce, I merely thought it would save you extra trouble and heartbreak. I—"

"No! No! Tell them." The last two words were aimed at Hamish, and that man, scarcely recognizable to Elspeth and Gran'pa, explained how he had already arranged for the burial to be here and now. Trying to justify her action and still hoping, Beulah approached Gran'pa Bruce, but he, having been through a similar heartbreak in his own life, took Bruce's side.

"Leave it be, woman. It matters nane where they lay her. She's wi' the Lord." So no more was said until Elspeth began to gather up Mary's belongings. The short funeral service was conducted by a stiff, somber Bruce MacAlister, hardly recognizable to anyone in attendance. The visitors, all except Peter, were preparing to leave when Hamish asked Elspeth what she thought she was doing.

"I'm taking the bairn until he's over it. Then we'll see."

"You'd better ask him first." None attempted to approach this Bruce, who had now relapsed into a state of extreme melancholy.

"But Hamish, he's not in a fit state to decide."

Gran'pa Bruce intervened again, "Too many folk wantin' to do the Lord's job for Him. We'll not take the bairn, Elspeth, unless Bruce says yes when you ask him." The answer echoed his previous one.

"No! She'll stay here!"

The boat waited at the landing, and the party were saying their farewells. As soon as they were safely aboard, Agatha no longer resisted the tears. Peter was staying anyway, and she didn't care who else saw her ravaged face. Silently and without reluctance, the group parted ways at the railway station.

$\mathcal{4}$

Peter strode up the path to the manse, every step showing his determination to finish this business of getting the highlandman back into living. First he would talk some sense into him and then. . . .

Hamish met him at the door: "I'm not lettin' onybody into his room 'til he gies the word!" And Peter, without resorting to violence, had to be satisfied for the time being.

Finally, with a quizzical glance at Bruce's self-appointed guardian, he asked, "What about you, Hamish Cormack? Tell me, what makes you so dedicated to the MacAlister? He never mentioned you when we were together in Glasgow or any of the times we spent at the croft in Aribaig. Nobody else there mentioned your name either."

"They're no' proud o' me there, even if I'm a changed creature, as Bruce says, although his grandfaither MacAlister believes I'm changed, too. I canna blame them at a', as there was a day when I wouldna' trust masel'. Ma ain faither, he wasna' at the funeral, but he's mairried to Elspeth; ye met her, too. She doesna' trust me yet, but ma faither is a believer in meeracles as I am noo. They all say I'm no' tae talk o' the times afore I ran away fae the Mains, but seein' you're his freen', maybe I'll tell ye o' it and then be done wi it." But Hamish stopped there.

After a few minutes of silence, Peter prompted him again, "Don't force yourself, Hamish, if speaking of it distresses you."

"Och, it's no' that, man. I chust thought I heard Mary's voice ootside. I dinna want her to ken o' it." Peter walked to the window, but nothing moved outside except the seagulls.

"It's not Mary Jean. Mrs. Gould took her for the afternoon, remember?"

"One day on the farm, when I was aboot seventeen and Bruce twelve, he was readin' oot loud fae a newspaper or some such. I never took much to the readin' an' writin', till Mistress Jean. Onyway, I wasna' interested in his readin'. I was mair interested in gettin' the siller oot o' yon kist in the front room. For a while I'd been plannin' to get awa'. Nay chance came tae get the money, so I was goin onyway. I ran oot the door tae the stable, gie angry at them a'. Bruce could do nothin' wrang, while I could dae nothin' richt.

"I got too close to a horse's hoofs in the stable, and it kicked me. I canna' blame the beast, as I had been mean to her mony times. I was still awfu' angry, so I took a whup and began tae leather the beast. Faither came oot and caught me at it. He yelled at me, and I somehow got the gun fae him, and it went aff. I thought I had kilt him, so I ran.

"My life fae then on I'll no' mention, chust that it was awfu' bad at times, until the nicht we went on the watter. Ye ken the rest o' that story."

Peter nodded. Yes, he knew, along with most of Scotland; and by the sound of the rumors, the story seemed to be having a resurrection. He wondered if that would be good or bad for his exasperating friend. Resolving that he would linger only a few more days to make sure the stubborn fellow would be all right, Peter reached in the box beside the front door and removed the walking stick he had noted there earlier.

"Your father recovered quickly from the incident, I take it?"

"Aye! Bruce tellt me he got ower it quick."

"I'll away for a hike then, Hamish. There's some braw scenery, and hiking's my favorite pastime. The scenery is bonny." Hamish nodded as he made his way to the kitchen.

"Aye. Elliott brocht a muckle ham. I'll set it to cookin'. We'll hae it for dinner at sundoon!" Recognizing an order and not a request, Peter strode out onto the heather. Might as well make the most of it. Maybe he would even leave on tomorrow's boat. His own practice called, and there was Agatha. He would need to do some coaxing with that young lady. They had wasted enough time.

Not even vaguely aware of the passing of day and night, living through the automatic acting out of habits accrued through a lifetime, Bruce MacAlister woke slowly. A dreamer in the throes of a terrible nightmare expects to wake up to relief and a resumption of happiness, but instead Bruce found the waking truth much more terrible than the nightmare.

A presence pervaded the room, causing the puzzled frown to deepen on his brow. Opening his eyes to the ceiling, he noticed the cross. Jean had remarked upon it once, saying it came from a bare place in the thatch on the roof.

I must tell the beadle about that. Next, to his mind and nostrils came a fragrance, Jean's scent, the kind he had asked her not to use on Sundays, for the benefit of the deacons and their wives. But that had been long long ago, in another life, before.

He tried desperately to avoid the full awakening he knew must come. His teeth, on edge with countless grindings, ached unceasingly. Clenching his fists where the nails had torn great, bleeding ridges on his palms, he burrowed them into his eye sockets, intent on blotting it out again—as if all or any of this would remove the terrible agony waiting to fill the emptiness.

"Bruce!" He acknowledged this by turning to face the wall.

"No, Bruce, lad, you've turned away ower many times already. Ye maun shake yoursel' now. Pick up the bits and start ower."

Shocked into a new awareness, he rolled onto his back and raised pain-flecked eyes to confirm he was hearing right. He wanted to assure himself that this was indeed Hamish Cormack laying down the law in such a familiar manner, as if. . . . Bruce struggled to sit up, but the effort proved too much, and he subsided again. Incredulity replaced all other emotions.

Hamish, waiting and watching patiently this long while for even a tiny spark of interest to ignite these eyes, grew tense now as the frosty blueness, dimmed by the unshed sorrow, trained on him unblinkingly. But he stared back, undaunted. Watching and listening, this past month, he had realized that something had snapped in his brother's mind. He seemed to think that they had only now been rescued from the drowning, and it was as if the two years in between then and the present had been wiped out.

Hamish had overheard the young doctor discuss it with Dr. Lockhart, and although the words were far beyond him, he had understood in part. Hadn't he shut out some of his own life for years?

Then Dr. Blair, from Glasgow, had told him what to do and say. "When he starts to come out of it, pretend at first he is waking from the drowning ordeal. We'll introduce him gradually to the true facts. I believe he'll come through it all right, after an interval. He's too thrawn and determined to wallow in this forever. However, should he still be in a dwam after, say six weeks, send for me again!" Hamish would send for nobody until he had tried a few tricks of his own, and he had Mary Jean.

He spoke carefully and slowly. "Aye! 'tis me. Hamish Cormack, sometimes afore kent as Hector Dermott. Since the Guid Lord saw fit to keep us baith alive, efter yon nicht in the watter, then I reckon what's left o' my life belongs to Him an' to you. As you were the one who risked yersel' to save my body, holdin' me up an keepin' us baith floatin', I ken ye couldna' hae done it withoot the Lord. You have to say the same. I'll chust stay here an' help ye and be yer servant for as long as I can!"

The long speech did nothing to dispel Bruce's shocked surprise, nor did it bring back the true events that had pushed him into this stupor. Such a state must have mercifully kept him from going over the rim into madness. He pushed the feather quilt to one side. Gently Hamish caught his hand.

"First ye have to eat somethin' mair nor that gruel we've been feedin' ye, on the young doctor's orders. I'll chust go and make some tea an' ham an' eggs!"

The effort to rise taxed his remaining strength, and Bruce sank back onto the pillows. A tentative hand explored his face to find a bristly beard, but he judged it to be no more than a day's growth. He must have been shaved. Further exploration revealed that although he wore smallclothes, he was spared the indignity of a nightshirt—a garment he had never in his life donned but had seen gracing many on their sickbeds, when he visited. Others wore them to their grave. He groaned aloud. Why did he have to come back to this horror? The groan had a different timbre from the countless sounds that had escaped him during the ravings he was recalling vaguely and reluctantly, although not yet fully aware of time's passing or events more recent than. . . . His being cried out for the darkness of ignorance to once more engulf him.

In spite of that yearning for more oblivion, he was coming out of it, and it must be faced. The whole scene etched itself onto his mind, never to fade completely, but eternal hope was coming alive again, and faintly the slow awakening began. A dark night of despair was over, and far to the East, dawn was breaking. God still reigned.

The door opened again to reveal Hamish carrying a loaded tray. Behind him stood Mrs. Gould, holding the hand of a child. An unmistakable tiny copy of his Jean, only with darker hair and light-gray eyes, instead of chestnut-brown ones.

The waking was to be complete. The child pulled her hand away and ran to the bed. "Daddy! Daddy! Mary wants Mammy."

Hamish set the tray on the table before proffering his arm as a lever. Acknowledging his weakness, Bruce grasped the arm and allowed himself to be pulled up. Meanwhile Mrs. Gould packed pillows in behind his head. Between them they settled Bruce to their mutual satisfaction in a manner confirming that they had performed this service many times before. The two servers, an unspoken truce uniting them because they had cared for this man and his motherless child, were intent on the moment. For weeks the strange household had functioned in limbo, waiting for the day now starting, when Bruce MacAlister would quicken to the world in which he now must live. The questions would come soon enough.

The first one was most irrelevant: "Who shaved me?"

"Och man, ye shaved yersel'. I chust held up the glass and the mug for ye."

The next question was more in keeping with the circumstances: "How long?"

"Five weeks."

"Five weeks! I've been lying here five weeks? My Lord!" The last words seemed more a moan than a prayer. Mary snuggled in beside him as Hamish stepped up to remove the tray.

Man, thought Hamish, *I hope we're not to have more of yon rantin' and ravin'.*

Bruce's next words assured him otherwise. "Tell me everything!"

Mrs. Gould slipped away, thankful that tonight she could go home to her own neglected house. Thinking that Hamish could manage fine now, she let out a long sigh of relief. The other parishioners had brought many offerings, and Hamish had accepted them as their due. New tatties and a bit turnip and some of the wee fancy cakes from Bella MacRae's oven, as well as a ham from her own Elliott, had been some of today's gifts.

Mary played with her dolls through the whole story. Not once during the telling did Bruce look at his child. If Hamish hesitated, Bruce opened his eyes, darkened again to sharp glaciers of pain, remembering, and signaled for the narration to continue. He must hear it all. At certain moments a faint smile crossed his lips, and he interrupted occasionally.

"Did I really say no to my mother and Granny Mac?"

"Aye, indeed, I was outside wi' Mary Jean, but yer shout reached my ears."

"It's a wonder they didn't overrule me."

"Ye sounded awfu' sure, and Dr. Peter and yer grandfaither sided wi' ye, so. . . ."

"Tell me that bit again. Granny Mac wanted to take Jean back to Glasgow for burial and—?"

"She did that, but you were thrawn, and Dr. Peter reminded her well, ye ken."

"Good for Peter, but I am surprised he considered me capable of making decisions."

"Whateffer! Afore he left, he gave me a long list o' dos and dinnas for you and Mary, as well as what to say when you came to yerself. That's by wi' noo!"

"You're just repeating Peter's instructions."

"No' awthegether. I do hae some gumption o' ma ain, as yer grandfaither told yer mither."

"What a pity I missed all that. Peter always had a way with Granny Mac, though, and Gran'pa Bruce could always handle Mam."

"A good thing, too, because you were swinging at her in yer anger. Yer grandfaither took you aside, and after saying I know not whit, came back to assure the group that the bairn would be well enough. He added that Mary should be here when you, as he said, came oot o' it."

Quietness reigned in the darkening room as Bruce allowed the meaning of Hamish's words to soak into his consciousness. That was Gran'pa, right enough.

Am I coming out of it then? he thought. *And if I am, do I want to? Where have I been all this time? I remember nothing of my sleeping and only snatches of my waking.* Shaking his head one more time, he uttered another irrelevance. "Where did they all sleep?"

"Well, Dr. Peter slept in the bed beside you. The ladies fae Glasgow stayed at the Johnstone's big hoose, and your mither stayed with the lady nurse, Mrs. Armstrong. Your grandfaither was up in the attic. We had mony a talk and—"

"You, Hamish. What about you?"

"Dinna fash yersel'. The Lord has all things under control. Ye might think that's a funny thing for me to say, and I've had

31

some struggles masel' aboot Mistress Jean, but somebody had to watch ye."

Silence returned for a while then.

"Why, Hamish?" They gazed at each other for a long moment. His stepbrother, who had, on his own admission, consorted with the dregs of humanity, looked not only into his eyes, but deep into his inner being. Both knew this *why* was not a repeat of the *why*s they had all asked of the Almighty the day Jean died.

"I have to. I dinna ken the *why*s. God has told me to help care for you, and Mary, too, until you can care for yourselves and each other. You've said it ower and ower again: 'God's ways are no' our ways.' "

Mary, hearing her name, jumped up from her play. Her father looked at her at last and immediately rejoined the ranks of her willing slaves. He sat for a while without speaking. Then, strangely humble, he addressed her, "Come here, my pet. I've some explaining to do!"

Rising from the stool, Hamish helped Mary Jean back up on the bed. Bruce had already moved, opening his arms to receive her.

Hamish had one problem: "The letters. I've sorted them in the order o' what I conseedered their importance. I'll go and get them. I'm that glad I can read an' write now."

"Yes, fetch the letters. We'd better get it over with."

Bruce spent the next few minutes gazing at his daughter, while she, big, serious eyes solemn, gazed back without a sound. Still slightly unsure, the child waited. Hamish returned.

"This envelope says two things. First, *Faculty of theology* and then *University of Glasgow*. I—"

"Open it, man! You're beginning to sound like Dugald, the postie at Aribaig."

Hamish obeyed, ending with, "It's signed with one word, *Alexander*."

"He is the Right Reverend Dr. A. A. Alexander. We tried many times to guess his other names. Rumor has it that one of them is *August*, but I think it more likely *Angus* or *Archibald*. We just called him 'Angry.' Read that bit again. I can't believe he's coming here!"

"Yes, here it is, 'So, unless I hear from you to the contrary, I will be arriving at your parish on Saturday, May 15. Excuse me if I cannot state the exact time until I get there. In Christ, Alexander.' "

"That's him, right enough. I wonder why he is coming here, unless they made him parish overseer after he retired as a theology professor." Hamish turned away. He had heard the rumors about the likely reason being the miracle again, but Bruce had enough to chew on for now.

"Why do we no' chust wait and see?"

"Right you are. Now, how soon is that, or should I say, what date is it today?"

"May the thirteenth, so that gies us two days. Maybe you should—"

"Yes, I'll get up now, but first I want to speak to Mary."

Without even the faintest of smiles, Hamish backed out of the small room.

Bruce began to address his daughter directly: "Now Mary, we'll need to make up for lost time, you and me. First I'll say I'm sorry for not being there to comfort you, my pet, when we lost your mammy. Please forgive me. I've been away in some far country of rebellion, but I've come back. After today, we'll talk no more of it. I dared to tell God our Maker—yours and mine and your mammy's too—that He made a mistake in taking away my Jean, your mother. Now, even if I'm coming to myself again, I still don't understand. Maybe I never will, but I do know this much. Your mammy has just gone ahead of us for a wee while. In the face of all eternity, not long at all! I'm assured that I have much to do here yet, before I can go to her, and so do you, wee Mary. That black night you were born and Jesus saw fit to save me out of the raging ocean, I made a vow never to complain and to work twice as hard, if He spared me. I forgot that promise for a while. But I've sulked long enough. The Bible says God loves the rebellious also, but I know the time has come when I'm to think and act as a man. Not just *any* man, at that, but *God's* man. And you, Mary darlin', I'll make it up to you, never fear."

Her eyes did not leave his face as he continued, "God is giving me another chance, and from now on I'll serve Him fully. I'll bring you up, with His help, in the knowledge and admonition of Him who, in His infinite wisdom, sees the end from the beginning—the source and giver of all life, even Jesus."

The child moved closer, and again Bruce gazed deep into the twin gray pools, flecked with a rich brown. Critics would say he imagined it, but he knew she understood. A knife shot through Bruce, but he held firmly to his resolve.

"I can tell you have all your mammy's winning ways, if not her red hair. Where did that dark mop come from, I wonder, and that wee pug nose? Don't be offended now; you're a braw lass, the bonniest I've ever seen, excepting your mammy. I've a feeling that your grannies and old Hamish recognize you're a beauty. But we're done with talking for the now, as we have some matters of business to attend to."

Mary spoke at last. "Mary wants dinner, Daddy!"

With perfect timing Mistress Gould appeared at the door, and Bruce nodded his consent as the kindly woman took Mary's hand. An all-too-familiar sound coming from below had captured his attention: a well-known voice that had roared and ranted, causing fearful, trembling undergraduates to wilt visibly, a voice that had also sometimes coaxed and cajoled discouraged students to carry on, a voice that had whispered sarcastically, a tone actually more dreaded by the seniors than the roaring. All this hid the inner softness that few ever witnessed and fewer credited.

"Still a mammy's boy, I see!" Instinctively Bruce clenched his fists in the old way, remembering that long-ago day when he had first heard the term referring to himself. A picture of that blackboard now rose in front of him, and he saw the "ten commandments" as they had appeared then. No answer was expected, so he awaited the inevitable.

"Ah, yes, so you've been hard hit, I'll grant ye that, but it's time to put aside mourning for the departed and start again in the business of serving the living."

Long years of habit still restrained Bruce from spitting out a bitter answer, but his thoughts were busy. *Trust old Angry to put into words what I, with the help of the Lord and Hamish, have only just resolved to do.*

The professor kept talking, ". . . Why it should be so, I know not. Anyway, to the business at hand and the reason I'm here. As you must know, it has taken an act of Parliament to restore to the congregations their right to choose their own minister. There's goin' to be some mixter-maxterin', let me tell you. A meeting for the purpose of voting is to take place. The folks of this parish might not want a big sissy who lies in his bed all day, mournin' what cannot be helped. Oh, I admit, and they have pity, too—don't look so offended—that you have had reason enough, up to a point, but that point has been reached, and I'll ask you one question: Do you wish to remain here in Inverechny?"

Bruce spoke his first word since his old mentor's entrance into the room, "Yes! That is, if they want me." His own lack of hesitation surprised him.

"I have to inform you they're on the verge of a disagreement; some want ye, some don't. I'm here to investigate certain rumors of miracle stories being spread abroad again about you and this place. General Assembly has heard of it, and the enquiry is to be reopened." A faint smile quirked Bruce's lips, to be quickly smothered. The tone of Angry's voice as he said, "General Assembly," suggested all should rise and a trumpet sound.

Roused to a question, he ventured, "What stories?"

The professor stared at him sternly, and the habit of years spoke for Bruce. "What stories, Dr. Alexander, sir?"

"Oh, thon ridiculous story of a miracle of you to have walked on water through a storm, carrying a man bigger than yourself! I managed to quench it at the time, but now, and with your wife dying so young, well it's come up again, as I said!" He snorted and waited for Bruce's denial, which did not come. "I recall coming over on the ferry with a crowd of folks who made the journey just to see you and the fellow you are purported to have rescued. I informed them then that it was rubbish. I trust you will stand up and deny it more soundly this time. It's now being said among your parishioners and others that your strange-sounding sermons are of the devil, and that's the reason God took your wife. They say, too, that you've turned into a raving maniac. Tell me, are you one? And what have you to say in your defense?"

Bruce laughed bitterly. "I've said nothing, and I won't say anything. What others might say I have no control over. As I told you at the time, it did seem that I gained more than the usual amount of strength needed to keep me treading the freezing water that dreadful night, but I have never considered it walking on water in that way. So much else has happened more recently and I. . . ." Bruce turned his head away. The memory searing him again was almost more than he could bear. Rallying, he continued, "I've heard of folks being given that extra surge of energy in moments of extreme urgency, and I believe that's partly what it was. As for the other accusations, I believe I'll answer them from the pulpit!"

"Good, I told the General Assembly much the same thing, but some of them didn't agree with me!" Again Bruce turned away, this time to hide a wider smile. How dared they not agree with Dr. Angry? The other man had more to say. ". . . So I will remain here until you are ready to resume your pulpit. I understand the man you rescued from the angry waves has been giving the sermons for the past weeks. God only knows what harm he may have done, and one of your parishioners sent word that you were unfit to shepherd any longer. We must now try to regain and, in our humble way, preserve some of the kirk's dignity."

"No doubt!" Bruce's sarcasm was lost on his superior as that man made for the door. Enunciating each word very carefully, so that Dr. Alexander could not mistake his meaning, Bruce called out to the retreating back, "Well, thank you, Dr. Alexander, sir, but I feel quite restored now. This Sunday I will mount my pulpit again."

Stooping to exit, the professor muttered the words so faintly that Bruce told himself he must have heard wrong: "Sorry, chieftain."

A snort of laughter escaped Bruce when he was once more alone. Imagine Hamish in the pulpit! What would his mother and the gang at Aribaig have to say about that? Oh, well, now Angry was here, and the dignity of the kirk would doubtless be restored. A promise he had made to himself on the day he knew for certain he would have a parish of his own came back to Bruce now, and before regrets assailed him again he repeated aloud: "I'll preach with dignity, God being my helper, I pray, but never again at the cost of joy." The vow was to prove prophetic. But at a price.

-·◦·❊{ 5 }❊·◦·-

Inverechny's wee white kirk was filled to overflowing, but with only the briefest of glances at the great Dr. Alexander, Bruce mounted his pulpit. Hamish opened the gate leading to the pulpit steps with a flourish, almost bowing the younger man into position. Earlier the beadle had read the day's lesson from the giant Bible placed high in its own special place in the sanctuary. Hamish might usurp some parts of the service, but not the "reading."

The crowd, and absently Bruce noted the delegation in sober black seated among them, settled back with a sigh. So he would sermonize on the Resurrection—always a fitting subject.

Bruce began at once to speak: "We have heard and noted the Word of the Lord as it described the meeting on the road to Emmaus. This meeting is set in time for us as we read of it being 'the same day'! The same day as what? Chapter twenty-four of the Gospel of Luke says it is still the first day of the week. So it is the same day the women went to the tomb to embalm the Lord's body, according to the custom. They found it empty. Shining strangers informed the women that Jesus would not be found there among the dead, as He was among the living. They said, 'He has risen as he promised!' " Bruce raised his arm to point to the empty cross outlined in the stained-glass window.

"The women had rushed to Peter's house, where the disciples were hidden, to tell them of their discovery. No one believed them, although Peter—and John, as his Gospel tells us—did go to see for themselves in the end. The others made tracks to resume their normal lives. Two of these are walking the seven miles home to Emmaus. The Bible doesn't have much to say about those two, except that they were discussing all that had transpired during the weeks just past. Suddenly the Lord appeared beside them and began asking questions about what they had been discussing so seriously. They did not recognize Him. I have heard many sermons on the subject of recognizing or not recognizing the Lord in our midst." Bruce stopped talking again, this time to glance out at his listeners. Not a sound could be heard as all eyes watched and all ears tuned in to his words.

"Sometimes I have taken on a load of guilt for myself and others as I have listened to sermons like that, but if you look again at the words in the chapter, it says, '. . . they were kept from recognizing him.' Who kept them from it and why? Could it have been the Holy Spirit? It must have been. I have heard the theory that the Lord Jesus, in gentleness, preferred not to embarrass His friends. I do not believe that altogether. He allowed them to speak their minds and hearts out; then He called them fools and unbelievers. I'm not making that up; here it is in verses twenty-four and twenty-five. Still they failed to recognize Him. It is not until they broke bread together that they were allowed to see Himself—and that only for a minute before He disappeared. Hear this!" Ignoring the sounds of protest from the black-clad listeners in the front pew, Bruce paused for breath.

"Jesus Christ, the Lord of Glory, even God incarnate, walked with them, talked with them, ate bread and meat with them, and they knew Him not! Then, the moment they recognized Him, He disappeared from their sight. All this is far beyond our feeble understanding. If some of us were to plan this, or even to write our own story about it, would we not tuck all the loose ends up a bit neater? Would we not have it all cut and dried, like yon seaweed out there on the wall or the peat from the bog? Oh, aye, I'm sure we would that! As it is we make our own mistakes, and we fail to recognize His Mighty Presence. The presence of the Holy Spirit, as Jesus promised the tarriers on Pentecost, would be their way of knowing Him. This is our way of knowing Him, too. He said He would still be with us always. He would be sending the Comforter."

Except for sounds of weeping among the women and a nose blowing here and there, the congregation sat silently. Bruce gazed about again. He closed his eyes for moments, as though listening to an inner voice, which indeed he was. He opened them again and resumed.

"As for me and mine. My wife is passed into His Full Presence. I know I kicked up a rare old stir when I realized it, and I still feel the want of her like a tearing of all that is in me—I always will until we are reunited—but I know now that He doeth all things well. I have made my peace with Him! The Word tells about mansions in glory and Himself goin' to prepare a place for us. That means for eternity. In that light then, our three-score years and ten, or whatever He allows us, is this much only. . . ." Bruce snapped his fingers.

"But we could not see things that way all the time, or we would not do our work here with as much zeal as we have to and as He needs us to. We are getting a fleeting glimpse the now, the same as the disciples got." Bruce allowed his gaze to move upward to the high, vaulted windows. Suddenly the place blazed with a new light. Tears glinted on almost every face, including some of the stern, craggy features of the jurors board, thinking of loved ones already gone. Women were frankly sobbing. The public pews at the back were filled to overflowing. A concerted sigh swept the building. The moment passed, and Bruce half turned to indicate his superior, with a wide sweep of his arm.

"Dr. Alexander is here to investigate, among other things, tales about the now-famed miracle." Angry groaned. Why could the young fool not stop here? He thanked God that most of those present could not see him behind the high fencing that surrounded the platform. "Dr. Alexander is one who would rather die than show a soft heart, but oh, make no mistake he's not a softy, far from it, as I know to my hurt!" The hand that would carry a scar and a tender place to Bruce's grave throbbed in response.

"But I want to explain to him and to my parishioners and to all here present; then it will be the one telling. If, after that, the kirk session still wants me as its minister, I'll stay. If it doesn't, then so be it! Our God reigns." Bruce proceeded to reiterate the true version of the night of the storm and his daughter's birth. He concluded with the latest catalog of accusations thrown at him from the recent troublemakers, accusations that spoke of the devil and his own. Bruce reminded all who listened that Jesus Himself had also been so accused.

By the time Bruce sat down, the hush was so deep you could touch it. This situation might have gone on if Mary, up until then happily playing, had not decided she wanted her daddy's attention. Her loud call broke the stillness, and the atmosphere changed. Bruce stopped to pick her up in his arms before he and Dr. Alexander walked together to the door to greet the people as they left. The day assumed a semblance of normalcy.

Hamish wailed. "My roast! It'll be a cinder!" Taking the private path to the manse, he raced away. Dr. Lockhart was loud in his praises, ignoring the presence of the dissenters, as he walked from the church to the manse.

"Magnificent sermon!" His own opinion that this man was a true man of God and should not be allowed to leave them was common knowledge in Inverechny.

Hamish's roast had not burnt to a cinder. Instead it was somewhat well done, but thoroughly enjoyable, as the table guests agreed later. The same verdict was announced from the kitchen table, where Hamish and the Goulds ate their share. The manse guests included Dr. Alexander and Dr. and Mistress Lockhart and, at Angry's specific request, Mr. and Mistress Johnstone.

It was the day of the decision. All the reports had been read, and Reverend Dr. Alexander had excelled himself in the concluding statement. Never had he spoken so eloquently and with such a depth of feeling. Greater therefore was the degree of shock when the results of the secret ballot were finally announced. The decision was worded: "The appointment of Reverend Bruce MacAlister to the living at Inverechny, on the Isle of Skye, in Scotland, will be terminated at the end of the parish year, viz. June thirtieth, in the year eighteen hundred and eighty."

"I fail entirely to see the joke. Perhaps you do not realize the seriousness of the situation or your own position, or perhaps you are still suffering from—"

"Not at all! No, forgive me Dr. Alexander, sir, you are right of course. It is no laughing matter, yet can you not see it? After all I've been through, serious as this situation no doubt is, it also can be overcome."

"What I see is you ostracized from the assembly and unable to secure a living in all of Scotland."

"Would that be so drastic, sir? Surely we must trust that the Lord is in control and His will shall be done in this matter."

The reverend doctor paid no heed but continued with his recriminations. "Such a disgrace must be shared by your teachers, you know. Only once before has a student of mine been thrown out, and his sin was unquestionably untenable." Nothing further was said, until Hamish, who had been listening outside the door for some time, stepped into the silent room to announce that tea was ready. For the first time Angus became aware of Hamish as a person. His earlier evaluation, based on the report of the miracle, underwent a complete reversal as he realized that now they had nothing else to lose. Forgetting his dignity for a moment, he took Hamish aside.

"Mister Cormack?"

Hamish bridled. "Och, reverend, man, I'm chust *Hamish*."

"Hamish, then. I'd like to hear your version of the night your boat overturned in the sea and all that's happened since."

"Aye?"

"As I'm sure all the others in the household have heard this betimes, maybe we could take a walk tomorrow morning, and you can tell me then."

"I'd have to take the time between making the breakfast an'—"

"I'm an early riser myself. Could we not go and watch the sunrise over the mainland, the glories of which I've heard so much about?"

"Och, aye, I'll ding on the door, then, chust afore daylight."

6

A stranger walk and talk seldom took place anywhere in all of Skye as secret arrangements were made between the unlikely schemers.

"Ye mean tae say ye'll trust me wi' all that siller?"

"Yes, of course, do you know of a good reason why I should not?"

"Plenty! Ask ony man in Lang Ford or Aribaig or even Portree, and he'll tell ye that Hamish Cormack, at times goin' by the name of *Hector Dermott,* put siller abune all else. Yet I've never kept mair nor one or two sovereigns on me at a time. Man, I dinna trust masel' wi' it."

Alexander looked keenly at this man, whom the Lord had seen fit to preserve, before answering, "All that is in the past, Hamish, before you near drowned. Remember, you are completely different now, since you seem to have found favor with God!"

"Aye, I do feel changed, an' that's a fact, but still I wouldna want to have all that siller on me at all."

"No, we'll take it to the post office and start a savings account in your name. Then you can go every week and take out what you need for the expenses. Should Bruce inquire, which I doubt he'll bother—his mind is so far away most of the time—tell him only that this is the Lord's way of providing for him until all is settled. I'll leave it to you to find a cottage in Mallaig or wherever he wants to be on the mainland. Presbytery won't throw you out, at least not 'til they get another minister, so you have ample time."

"What if he doesna' want to go to Mallaig, an what if—"

"Just take each day as it comes, Hamish. The Bible says ' . . . sufficient unto the day is the evil thereof.' " But Hamish no longer listened.

"And what if the folks here in Inverechny willna' let him go? As weel as liking him an' his preachin', as some o' them do, the folk in the shops and the inn as weel as the ferryman are fair pleased wi' all the business the summer visitors bring these days. Did ye ken a mannie wi' the name o' Cook brought a trainload from England on a trip to the sound? They call it the miracle cruise."

"I keep telling you, Hamish, to let each day bring its own troubles and solutions. Maybe it's here in Inverechny you should be looking for a cottage, but I'm sure the publicity will die down as time goes on."

Hamish emitted what sounded like a growl. He was still far from understanding what had happened. His natural feelings rebelled against being rushed into something out of his own control. He thought of one last argument. "What aboot yon Johnstone. He's fair got it in for Bruce!"

For a minute Alexander looked puzzled, then his brow cleared. "Have no fear, my man. Right shall prevail over might, and your Bruce has the right." Far from satisfied but with no more arguments, Hamish subsided.

Retracing their steps through the village, both men were silent, each busy with his own thoughts. While walking on the high moor, Hamish had shown the other man the spot where Bruce had spent his night of black mourning. Dr. Alexander murmured, "Them that go forth weeping shall return in the morning bearing precious seed and shall come again rejoicing." Hamish did not know what he meant.

Suddenly Hamish stopped and pointed toward the sea. His unlikely companion waited politely, but even after the lapse of time Hamish could not express his feelings properly as he tried to describe the storm. The peaceful lapping water gave the lie to his words.

"Och, I dinna ken how it happened. I only ken I should be drooned efter a nicht in yon cauld watter, an' I'm alive and hale. I'll be God's servant, an' Bruce's as well, for all the days o' my life. Noo that Jean's awa', he'll need me mair than ever."

Bruce saw them coming from a long way off. He was standing in the tiny garden between the manse and the kirk, gazing up toward the moor. Mary Jean played at his feet. Every few minutes he would glance at the child, a strange smile playing on his face. He saw Jean, the beloved, in her child, and he was ready to accept that also as a gift from God.

Alexander had a strange question for Hamish before they reached the garden. "Is the child like her mammy?"

Hamish shook his head. "She's like hersel'." He disappeared toward the kitchen door to begin his day.

Later that morning Lachlan brought a letter from Strathcona House, addressed to Bruce in a very childish script. Handing it over at table, Hamish waited for him to read it. With a puzzled frown, Bruce slit the envelope then immediately passed it back to Hamish.

"Read it out, Hamish."

"Dear Master Bruce: The mistress is pining and not just for Miss Jean. She's that worried aboot everybody up there. She'll not eat, and Cook and me don't know what to do, so I put pen to paper to ask your advice, then wait for your answer. Yours truly, Betsy Degg and Cook MacLaren. P.S. How is wee Mary Jean? B.D."

"Hamish, is Dr. Alexander still about?"

"Aye, he's admirin' the rhododendron buds. Will I get him?"

"No, I'll find him myself." Alexander was amazed to be handed the simple letter, but he read it obligingly and waited.

"What do you think of that, Dr. Alexander, sir?"

"It seems very sad, but what does it have to do with me?"

"I have many things to see to before I can go to Glasgow.

Would you be so kind as to take a message to Granny Mac? She's my late wife's grandmother and the lady referred to in the letter as the mistress. Break it to her that I'll be leaving here, but soften it by telling her I'll be bringing Mary Jean to Strathcona House before we settle in Aribaig for the winter. I'll be writing in the next day or two, but if you could do that, it will ease the poor soul sooner."

The professor's first reaction was to refuse. "It won't be good news I bring about your dismissal." A glance at the granite face of his never-to-be-admitted but always-favorite pupil changed his mind promptly. "Write it down, with directions and instructions."

7

On the day following Jean's funeral, just before he and Elspeth had left to board the ferry for Mallaig, Gran'pa Bruce MacAlister had also drawn Hamish Cormack aside. It was the first time since the shooting, fourteen years before, that the two had been alone together to talk. Neither of them had mentioned that terrible day, and the older man quickly concluded that Hamish, being indeed a new creature, had no real remembrance of it.

Thinking, *So be it,* he silently thanked the Lord for the promise of God that says, "Forgetting that which is behind. . . ." He approached Hamish with a request, fully assured that the Holy Spirit had done a complete work in Andrew's son.

Alone with Hamish in the tiny kitchen, after congratulating him, Gran'pa had spoken: "I'm glad you're learning to read and write English, Hamish, lad!"

"Aye, well, I canna write it too weel yet, but Mistress Jean learned me every day."

"Will ye send us a letter to Aribaig once a week then, wi' all the news about the bairn and Bruce? I don't suppose he'll be doin' any writin' his own self the now."

"Aye, I will, every week." The conversation had ended there.

Faithfully then, every Sunday afternoon, as soon as the dinner dishes were washed up, Hamish had taken up the writing pad and pencil and with thoughtful deliberation pondered his latest missive. They seldom varied:

Dear all:

I hope this finds you as it leaves us, and that is well enuff. He is just the same, and wee Mary Jean is sonsy, and me I tell the folk in the kirk aboot the nicht on the watter and that I'm saved. Some want tae argy, but A just say A know it is so cause I'm no drooned and I'm a changed man.

Your son,
Hamish Cormack

Gran'pa could scarcely hide his mirth as he had read the first letter aloud, but Bruce's mother had not smiled.

" 'He's just the same' could mean anything. When I think of him lying there and the wee lass at the mercy of Hamish, and why does he go on aboot the miracle? That's all past and done with and better forgotten. Och, it doesn't bear thinking about."

"Now, wife, we're not goin' to start that again, and you're not bein' fair. Hamish is a changed man, and he'll let no harm come to Mary. He's come a long way since the time you speak of. You and Gran'pa both witnessed that at the time of Jean's funeral. His letters are not fancy, but they tell us they're all as well as we can expect for the now. Besides that, the neighbor women are keepin' a watch on things."

"It's not the same! They should be here with us, or I should be there with them."

Gran'pa had spoken up then: "Elspeth, lass, we've talked about all that, and it's best to leave things the way they are. With our prayers and in God's good time the healin' will come."

So the letters had continued to arrive at the croft each week. With minor variations, the letters told the same thing. 'He's fine, and Mary's sonsy." One week there was a change.

Gran'pa, with Melancholy trotting beside him, walked out to meet Dugald. The dog's ears stood erect as Gran'pa spoke. "Aye, Melly, old girl, I've a feelin' the day's letter is different. Maybe we'll have some real news this week." Melancholy wagged her tail vigorously. Elspeth, pretending to shake a dustless mat, waited on the step.

The first sentence was the same as usual, and Elspeth poured the tea, her interest waning.

"Dear all: I hope this finds you as it leaves us, and that is weel enuff." The reading stopped, and everyone waited for it to resume. "Praise God!"

"Did he write that?"

"Och, no. I'm saying that, and so should you. Listen!"

"He came out o' it yesterday. He ett ham and eggs and scones, and he had a long blether wi' the bairn. The neebur women and me are that pleased. He preached this morning, and I didna need to speak. That iss good. I've not much more to say. Maybe he will rite his own self next week. O aye, the big doctor, Angry as he ca's him, has been here. Your son, Hamish Cormack."

Elspeth's happy tears began to flow as she cried, "Thank God, oh, thank God, maybe now Bruce'll—"

"Yes, we should thank God, and we do, but we must wait now, Elspeth. We'll not interfere or offer suggestions until he asks us."

"I know, Gran'pa, but I do so want to see the bairn and to make sure for myself they are well enuff as Hamish says, and maybe I'll ask Andrew if—"

"Ask Andrew what, wife? Is the tea cauld? And I thought I heard Melly shoutin' at Dugald. Has somethin' different come fae Inverechny the day?"

"Yes, Andrew. Hamish's letter says there's a change. Gran'-pa'll tell you about it while I make more tea."

Andrew's reaction echoed their earlier one.

"Praise the Lord, and here's my good news. I got top prices for yon lambs yesterday, and maybe there's just enough siller in the kist to buy a ticket for a certain granny to pay another visit to a certain manse on the Isle of Skye!"

"Oh, Andrew!" wailed Elspeth, and the men exchanged knowing glances as the joyful tears overflowed.

{ 8 }

So it happened that Elspeth Cormack was seated proudly in the manse pew with Mary Jean when her son, Reverend Bruce MacAlister, gave his final sermon to the congregation of Inverechny. Her happiness, when she heard that Bruce was returning to normal, faltered only slightly when she learned that he would be leaving his parish. The combined facts that session had asked him to leave because, one, they suspected he had falsified a miracle, and two, that having lost his wife, he had also lost his mind, apparently never dawned on Elspeth. Why, in less than three short years Bruce had come from raw curate to mature minister, from newlywed to widower, father of the motherless little girl now nestled contentedly at her granny's side and holding tight to her new doll.

Risking a hasty glance round, Elspeth soon realized that the pews behind her were full. The prayers ended, and the Scripture reading began. Bruce had chosen a few verses from the thirteenth chapter of the Book of Acts. There followed the responsive reading, Inverechny's only concession to Psalm 100's admonition to "make a joyful noise unto the Lord."

No sound, joyful or otherwise, accompanied Bruce as he climbed the steps to take his place in the pulpit.

"Beloved—that includes all among us here who fear and reverence God—it is to us this message of salvation has *now* been sent! For the people of these islands set in the sea and the

51

rulers of the synagogue—in this case the Kirk of Scotland—have refused to recognize God's miracles for today. But we are not discouraged. Again a parallel can be seen. Our Lord Jesus had a similar one. In fact many far worse things happened to Him. If the rulers in those days refused to believe the Lord of Glory, naming Him a madman when He walked the earth in person, accusing Him of blasphemy and of calling Himself holy and Son of God, even though He was Himself God, who are we to expect better treatment? None could have been more amazed than I, or as you seem to have been, when the Lord Jesus chose us to show His power through. Far be it then from me and my brother, Hamish, to put ourselves on a level with Paul or Barnabas, let alone the Lord, but all who profess the Word of God must know how the Holy Spirit blows where He will and uses whom or what He finds available to achieve His purpose. His purpose is to spread the Gospel, my friends!"

Keeping her eyes on Mary, but concentrating on her son's address, Elspeth could not decide whether to be proud of him or more concerned. If the question had arisen, she would have conceded that his form of speaking could be likened to that of their friend Fraser Clegg, the one-time minister of Aribaig, but there any resemblance to Fraser, or any preacher she had ever heard, ended. When Bruce, after emphasizing the word *now*, used the term *islands of the sea*, she recognized that it was true. He did consider the sea episode to be a present-day miracle, with himself a vessel of proclamation. Stealing another glance at the man Johnstone, Bruce's chief antagonist, according to Hamish, she began to quake inside for her son. Bruce's jaw and lip could have been set in stone, so awesome did he appear. Worse was to follow.

"I look round at you all and question why some of you are here. If you are here to worship God and to wonder at His marvelous works that we're telling of, then a hundred thousand welcomes to you, but if you came to gaze at my brother and me as a circus act, then see you do it not! We are only human beings, like yourselves. Turn away from seeking miracles and unusual spectacles, and seek the Living God. The good news that Jesus is alive should thrill you much more than the fact that we survived that black night of storm. That He is risen as He said is all that really counts. He was alive before any other thing was, and He lives forever. Someday He's coming again, and we must be ready for that great day. Amen!"

The crowd sat on in mummylike silence. Bruce bent his head in prayer; then, in a more subdued manner, he began again to speak.

"Inverechny has been like the waters of Mara to me—both bitter and sweet. My feelings, as I stand before you in this pulpit for the last time, also hold that mixture of emotions. However, uppermost this very minute is the taste of sweet. I have been through the bitter gall of losing my dear wife, having had her for such a short time, and then the further bitterness of being dismissed from my living here, accused, among other things, of being unstable in my ways. But I can say in truth I am glad the Holy Spirit has again turned the bitter to sweet. I was pleased to answer the call to Inverechny and would have been equally glad to continue in servanthood here, but I consider the Lord to be decreeing otherwise for me.

"To my mother, whose heart's desire to see me an ordained minister may seem to have been granted for a short time, only to be snatched away, I publicly ask her forgiveness for that and also for what I am about to say. The Kirk of Scotland may have expelled me and banned me in every parish within its jurisdiction, for the time being, but it cannot take away my ordination. However, if I cannot preach in this denomination, such ordination is worth little. I say 'Praise the Lord!' I am free to present my message in all its fullness, without apology or compromise. God chose this people to show the way, but the rulers spurned it, as in Paul's day. Now watch as we go out into the highways and byways.

"We will begin in a small town on the mainland, Aribaig, where I grew up. Beyond that, we'll go as the Macedonian call directs—in this case the Caledonian call! Indeed the Lord has commanded us to do so. Again, without apology or false humility, I echo Paul's words. Long have I had the vision to reach the sea isles surrounding our own Scotland, and the opportunities are falling into place to answer the call to 'go over to help them.' Fully convinced I am that it is God who calls me. 'Help them do what?' you may well ask, and I will answer here and now. 'Believe in the Lord Jesus Christ, and you shall be saved, you and your household!' "

"Don't fret, Mam, it'll be well. You'll see. The devil meant it for evil, but our God will turn it all into good." But Elspeth refused to be comforted. Three times in his life Bruce had defied her by doing something she strongly disapproved of, and this time she knew Andrew would agree with her. The conflict had reached the point in her mind where she no longer wished to talk about it. If thoughts of her father's harsh way of dealing with conflict crossed her mind, she smothered them quickly.

Their talk was taking place the day after Bruce had opened his innermost being to his congregation. Elspeth was preparing to leave for Aribaig, and Bruce would escort her to the boat. She had not responded to his remarks, so he tried again. "I'm sorry if I've offended you, Mother, but I'm not sorry for what I said on Sunday. It had to be done. Would you prefer me to tell lies?"

"Of course not, but you could have been more discreet. For instance, did you have to rub it in about the presbytery in public? In case you didn't notice, the laird himself was in the pew along with that Mr. and Mistress Johnstone. Oh, Bruce, you were downright insultin' to some of these folk!"

"Mother, I'm surprised at you. I never thought of you as a snob, noticing the rich folks and the gentry. They are just as curious as the more-ordinary beings. Anyway, as long as I speak the truth, does it matter what the Laird of ClanRanald, or any other earthly laird, thinks of me? As for the Johnstones, well, I don't—"

"Son, you've still an awful lot to learn, in spite of your big words. Certainly I might be considered a snob, but mind that

Jesus loves them, too, and we're not to scorn them, anymore than the poor and the needy, especially not out in front of the whole kirk."

"I'll grant I've a lot to learn, but I must speak the words as the Lord gives them to me. Pray that anything insulting that was not edifying will be overlooked. Now, if you want to catch the ferry the day, we'll have to go."

"Let me take another wee look at Mary, first. I'll agree with your prayer, Bruce, but my biggest worry is not so much what has been done as what you'll be doing now—traipsing off about the country, with only you and Hamish and that Gypsy caravan. I don't think. . . ." She choked and turned away. They had discussed this thoroughly, and she knew the futility of trying to change his mind.

Full of compassion, Bruce reached over and gripped her hand. "Oh, Mam! We'll not travel the isles in the winter, but we'll stay either at Aribaig or Glasgow. Will that please you?" Elspeth brightened visibly.

"Oh, aye, son. Yes, indeed! That'll please me some but—"

"All right. You have taught me many times, you and Gran'pa and Andrew, no futile regrets. I know in my spirit that in my time of deepest distress, when I would not heed the Lord's own voice, I remembered your teaching and theirs, and that helped me through. One at a time is good fishin', as Gran'pa says. Now should we not give thanks before you go?"

"We should. Thank you, Lord. Now when can I tell Gran'pa and Andrew you'll be coming?" Bruce laughed aloud, and his mother's heart gladdened further at the sound. Maybe things were not so bad.

"Hamish'll need to be consulted about all that. I have a month or so to get ready before the new minister comes to take possession of the manse. In the meantime I believe a locum will be coming over from the mainland for the Sundays only. Then Hamish and I will need to earn our way, like Paul with his tent making. I don't know how Hamish has got by so far, but—Oh, I must practice what I preach about one day at a time. Here's the ferry, Mam." Elspeth finished pulling on her gloves, admiring as always the fine pigskin. Nice gloves were her one indulgence, she thought, and oh, she was procrastinating again. Picking up her small reticule, she stepped through the barrier where only those boarding could go.

"Good-bye then, son. Watch the bairn!"

"Good-bye, Mam, and try not to worry about us. We'll look after each other—and Mary Jean, too."

"But meenister! I'm sent here tae tell ye, and Elliott here's my witness, along wi' the Lord Hissel', that we, the majority o' parishioners o' Inverechny, the verra folk who appointed ye to come, are ready and willin' to staun' behind ye and defy the presbytery to keep ye in oor manse and oor kirk." The deputation of two, consisting of Lachlan MacLachlan and Elliott Gould, had arrived just as Bruce and Hamish had finished eating their dinner.

Hamish, sensing something solemn and important, had quickly cleared the table before taking up his vantage point in the small lobby between the rooms. He held his breath, waiting for Bruce to answer. The offer was a tempting one. Silence told Hamish more than words that Bruce was praying.

In his own way Hamish prayed also. "Oh, my Lord. Let him say the richt thing. It would indeed be easier for us a' if he agrees to bide here, but again we have oor plans made to flit, and they're good plans."

The minutes ticked away. Hamish had brought a tray with tea and biscuits, but the tray lay untouched on the table by the hearth. All at once Bruce spoke: "Elliott, and you, too, Lachlan, please take no offense at what I am going to be saying to you now." From his vantage point Hamish sighed with relief as the beloved voice continued, "There it is then. I could not stay in such circumstances. My child and I could not rest easy under this cloud of banishment from presbytery that hangs over us. You say *majority*, meaning some do not agree, and I do not blame them. I have had periods when I did not believe certain miracle reports myself. As for my way of reacting to the news of my wife's passing, well, Lachlan, you saw and heard that. And you, Elliott, know all about the way I carried on. *Sensible* would not be a way of describing it. In fact they are correct in saying I was demented in my sorrow." Bruce gazed into the fire.

"God's Word says we must submit to those in authority over us, and I bow to that. The kirk's history is rank with splits and dissension, and I want none of that. It's thanking you I am, though, for your vote of confidence in my work here. It is all by the grace of God, if my words and my actions have found favor and been blessed with fruit for the Kingdom in the long run. That's all the reward I need." He choked a bit on the last words.

Elliott, who had been standing by without comment to this point, said, "It's a cryin' shame, that's what it is. A body has reason to go a bit daft when his—" A warning cough from Lachlan made him change his mind. "We canna' help wonderin'. What will ye do, and where will ye go, if the kirk willna hae ye now?"

"I will continue to preach the Gospel as long as I live. Where? Well, that is in the Lord's hands!"

Aye an' in mine, too! thought Hamish as he quickly moved away from the door. *If things were left in your hands, Reverend Bruce MacAlister, you an' the bairn, an me, too, would go gye hungry.*

The visitors prepared to leave as Bruce still talked: "Through the Lord's provision and the good stewardship of my brother, Hamish, we have been able to procure a most cleverly contrapted caravan. It's fitted out like a wee castle inside an'—" He got no further.

"Ye mean tae tell us, meenister, that ye intend to live in a tinker's caravan—and with wee Mary, too?"

"Indeed and I do, Elliott. Mary Jean will go where I go."

Lachlan picked up the argument. "It's no' fittin' for a meenister o' the kirk! Maist undignified."

"Fortunately for the kirk, then, I am no longer answerable to presbytery as one of their ministers or to the kirk session of Inverechny parish." Bruce had lost his patience. "Now if you will excuse me, gentlemen, Hamish and I have a lot to do to get ready for the flitting."

Elliott lingered on the step for a parting word, "Ye'll bring Mary to see the wife and me afore ye go?"

Bruce placed a hand on the kindly man's shoulder and answered with one word: "Aye!"

9

Andrew awaited his wife at the ferry landing. After he helped her climb into the box cart, she began at once to give him all the news.

"Hold on there, wife, are ye tellin' me that he's not a meenister o' the kirk now?"

"Oh, Andrew, we know he'll always be a minister, but for the time being, yes, he has been expelled from the kirk. What'll happen after they hear of last Sunday's sermon I dread to think."

"Has he truly gone daft, then, like they're sayin'? Has his wife's passin' an all the other happenchances turned his mind?"

"No, no, in fact he has come a long way since the time of the funeral. But he doesn't care what folk think now. Like saying, 'What can they do to me that's any worse than what's happened already?'"

Andrew searched her face closely before replying, "You're not too upset then, Elspeth, lass? After all the years of hoping and working to make him a minister o' the kirk?"

"Och, I'm a good deal upset, but I can see how if he hadn't wanted to be a minister nobody could have made him one." She laughed suddenly. "He can fair preach, I'll grant him that. A pin could be heard if one had dropped in that service." The horse, Elijah, knowing the way, plodded on, and the two in the box cart sat quietly for some distance, swaying to the motion of familiar bumps and ridges.

"What about you, Andrew? What are you thinking of what I've been telling you?"

"We've all worked for that goal, lass, and I would not be truthful if I said I liked all this straying from the ordinary way of doing things. However, I'll get over it. I never was one to say a thing muan be right because it's aye been done that way. There's a lot to be said for the tried and true, as long as it stays true. Fraser Clegg had some different ideas o' his own, too, but he never offended the established kirk, that we ken of, by expoundin' on them fae the pulpit. It's a pity sometimes that the hard way is the only way some of us find our road in life. Our Bruce is a man, and inside he'll always be a minister, and well, he knows what he's in for now, so we'll not say more."

"They'll be staying here with us for some of the winter months, and they'll come for a few weeks before they set out on this 'crusade.' Will that be all right, Andrew?"

"Aye, that will be more than all right, wife. We'll get to see the bairn, and this granny'll not be so worried." Again his quizzical glance searched her. "We want no hard feelings, Elspeth. Ye've suffered enough from hard feelings."

"You're a good man, Andrew Cormack. You and Gran'pa Bruce. I don't know how we would have managed at all without the both of you." This time she did not turn her head but returned his gaze, blue eyes brimming.

"Now! Now! The Lord would have provided others, if we hadn't been handy at the time. We'll see the whole business mair clearly by and by. I'm still conveenced oor lad has great exploits to do for the Lord. Like the guid book says. 'The half has never yet been told.' If they're comin' for the winter, we'll have to do some expandin'. His attic room'll not hold him an' the bairn, I'm thinkin'."

Elspeth shook her head, and her voice quivered slightly as she said, "He'll be bringing the caravan!"

They were silent for a while until suddenly Andrew pulled on the reins. "Whoa!"

Elspeth stopped dreaming and gazed at him again.

"What about you paying some attention to your own man here for a change? We've missed ye, ye ken!" Astonishment rounded Elspeth's mouth into an O, but more was to come. "He's goin' his own gait, our son, and we canna change a thing about it, even if we wanted to now. You an' me, we're not so auld that we have to go into a decline or whateffer they call that. What I'm sayin' is this: We've some extra siller in the kist. The market is still up, and I sold a stirk yesterday. Gran'pa can get two village lads to help him whilest you an' me go jauntin'. Nae arguments, the head of the house has spoken!"

"Why, Andrew! Andrew! I couldn't argue even if I wanted to. I'm fair stricken dumb. Are ye sure I—"

"Chust like a wumman, she says she's stricken dumb, an' she'll no' argue, then she starts to argue. Ye think I'm off ma head, but I'm not. Not a'thegither, although when ye look at me like that—Well, anyway, we're goin' for a holiday and not afore time. What do they fancy books ca' it then?"

Half laughing, half crying, Elspeth found the word: "*Honeymoon!*" Feeling no pressure on the reins, Elijah decided to sample the grass by the roadside. No one stopped him.

10

The small news item, almost hidden on an inside column of the *Times*, did not rate a bold headline, but it did cause a variety of reactions around the country.

In Glasgow Peter Blair read it aloud to Mr. Bennett after the article had been brought to their attention by Mistress Oliver when she carried in their tray of coffee and biscuits.

"Excuse me, Mr. Bennett, but I thought you, and maybe the doctor here, would be interested in this!" George handed the folded newspaper to Peter.

" 'Miracle Preacher Defies Kirk Government,' Well, well! It's about our highland laddie!"

"Will you please read it, boy?" George's tone gave away his unusual impatience.

A young preacher, little more than a curate, challenged the leaders or, in his own words the rulers, of the Kirk of Scotland in a farewell address to his congregation this past Sunday. One suspects a slight case of sour grapes as the aforementioned minister had just been expelled from his parish living in the town of Inverechny on the Isle of Skye.

Before giving the sermon in question, Reverend Bruce MacAlister had been accused by the kirk, among other things, of having falsified reports of a miracle. Any chance of reinstatement vanished when MacAlister, before about two hundred most-attentive listeners, charged the kirk assembly with being despisers of God's Word. This writer, in conversation with a parishioner and a close neighbor of the manse, learned that the ex-minister will take to the road—or is it the sea lanes round about the islands?—as a traveling preacher. The term *Gypsy caravan* is being bandied about to describe the rebel's future manse. What happened to the miracles now?

"Well! Imagine that! Good for our hielan' laddie! But man, what will he do now? That's what I'd like to know." Peter was on one of his frequent visits to the home of George Bennett. They met to discuss details of the report George was preparing for social reformer Charles Booth, but more recently, their talks had centered less on Booth's polls than on Bruce MacAlister's doings and as George so quaintly phrased it, how the Lord was leading that young man.

"Read it again, Peter. I cannot take it in! We've learned not to believe all we read in the papers, you know. Remember that hoax about the circus last year? All lies!"

"Yes, but who would gain from this story here? The fire hoax attracted crowds of people to the circus for weeks after."

"Just a minute. Read that bit about the neighbor again. I wonder. . . . " George glanced apologetically at Peter, who finished the sentence, "You wonder if it's time. I do, too. Remember I said there was nothing to be done until he came out of it, and now, judging by this, he has come out of it completely. He's his own man again."

George nodded. "I agree with you here and now, as I did when you came back from Jean's funeral, in that you did all you could. I meant no criticism. According to Beulah, nobody's been able to do much."

Peter pointed toward the paper. "Aye! I see what you mean. Strathcona House will have the true story, no doubt. Surely that reporter made it up about a caravan." The two looked at each other; then Peter jumped to his feet, narrowly missing upsetting the coffee tray.

"I'm for Strathcona House. Are you coming?"

"Hold on, and I'll order the carriage."

A delighted Betsy opened the door to them. "Oh, yes, the mistress is at home to you. I'll tell her you're here."

Beulah raised her hand to acknowledge the announcement. "Show them in, Betsy!"

"Shall I bring more tea, mistress?" The maid was avid for all the news.

"Of course, Betsy." To the visitors, "How are you, George, and you, Dr. Blair?"

"More important, how are you, Beulah? But we did not rush over to exchange polite talk today." George waved the newspaper. "We want to find out firsthand what really happened in Skye."

"Wait a minute. How did you know I've just had a special-delivery letter from Skye? It only arrived about an hour ago."

Peter could not resist saying, "Oh, our Bruce is quite the celebrity. We read it in the *Times!*"

Incredulity registered on Beulah's face, and George took pity on her. "Peter's exaggerating. This short item in the paper concerns Bruce. That's what he means."

"I see, and what did the *Times* have to say about Bruce?"

"We don't believe all that's in the paper. We only agree that something must have instigated the report. The miracle story we already knew about, but that happened more than two years ago and should no longer be news, unless what is going on up there now casts some devious aspersions upon Bruce's character. Anyway we wanted your version."

"May I see the newspaper, if you please?"

"Well, I don't think anything very bad has been said, maybe a few facts twisted. Could we hear what he has to say for himself?"

"Dr. Alexander came to visit me, you know, and Bruce's old professor is on his side. I learned many things in our short conversation. Some things I'm pledged never to reveal, but don't worry, they are all to the good of our Bruce."

For the next hour Beulah relayed the happenings of the past three months in Inverechny. Her listeners sat in silence for the most part, and when Betsy, after setting down the fresh pot of tea, stood at the door to listen in, no objections were raised. A choking sound came from the maid when Beulah repeated the part about Mary Jean.

"Her hair is changing to a dark brown, and her eyes are a most uncommon gray color, but you'll see for yourself when we come to Glasgow," Beulah read.

"They're coming to Glasgow? Oh, mistress." Using her apron to dry her tears, Betsy rushed back to the kitchen. She and Cook MacLaren had a lot to talk about.

George smiled in the direction of the departing maid. "When are they coming, Beulah, my dear?"

"September sometime." Beulah dabbed at her eyes. "I don't know if I can face him. Some of the things I said to him at the funeral."

"Granny Mac," Peter interrupted. "Let me assure you from a strictly medical point of view, that Bruce has no recollection whatsoever of the time we were at Inverechny, nor will he recall any of the conversations. Everything he said and did during those first few weeks came from automatic responses or instinct. The 'New Thought' teaches us—"

"Never mind the 'New Thought' just now, Peter," George broke in. "Beulah, my dear, the Word of God teaches forgiveness to the nth degree. Bruce MacAlister is committed to that Word above all else. He may have lost his way for a while, but God's hand was and still is upon him. We'll be ready to welcome them with open arms and hearts. May our dear Lord give them Godspeed!"

-•⇥{ 11 }⇤•-

In Edinburgh Jimmy Ballantyne whistled as he pushed the *Times* through the letter box of number 24 Westercrofts Road. He was near the end of his round, and today was payday. Besides, his big sister worked here, and she always had a "piece" for him.

Rosie heard him as she put the finishing touches to Mistress Munro's breakfast tray. He was early this morning, and she'd forgotten his treat. Oh, well, too late now. A wee sprig of lilac in a posy bowl, then the paper, and Mistress Munro's tray was ready. Maybe today she would notice.

"Thank you, Aggie." Even after all these years, the mistress still called her maids Aggie.

Rosie never allowed this to go unnoted, so she said, "I'm Rosie Ballantyne, Mistress Munro, and here's your paper. That cheeky Jimmy brought it early for once, so you can enjoy it wi' your tea."

"Yes, Rosie, I will. Did the postman come?"

"Not yet, mistress. I'll bring the letters up as soon as he comes. I'm away now to do the washin'. Just ring if you want anything else."

"The tray is very nice, and I won't need anything else."

Sipping the hot, sweet tea, Margaret Munro idly turned the paper over. Hugh was right about some things. Before "it" happened, he had always declared how scandalous it was to

66

have all that advertising in beside the news. Why even her favorite marmalade that she was nibbling on now had its picture above the news columns. Suddenly a familiar name leaped out of the page at her.

Steady, Margaret! she told herself. *There's thousands of MacAlisters in Scotland, even in Skye, and many hundreds of Bruce MacAlisters. Surely if it's our Bruce, Elspeth, although she doesn't write that often, even now, would have told you.* She rang the bell.

"Rosie, tell me if I'm seeing right. Does that say Reverend Bruce MacAlister?"

"Aye, it does, Mistress Munro. Should I read it out to you?"

"No, no! Just take the tray away. I'm going to get up. I'll have a lot to do today. Where's my box?"

Over the years the box had accumulated a pathetic collection of keepsakes, mostly letters from the original Aggie in Arbroath. Until recently the faithful old servant had penned a few words, posting a letter fairly regularly every month. Then one day the handwriting had been different, and one of Aggie's many nieces had informed Margaret that Auntie's rheumatics were so bad now she could no longer write, although her tongue was as sharp as ever. Margaret had smiled sadly at that. She could see in her mind the whole scene of a frustrated Aggie being dependent upon others after a lifetime of serving. Once in a while the letters had contained scraps of news about Elspeth. Elspeth had written to Aggie every year at Christmastime, knowing the news would be passed on in such a way as to ensure her mother would not be punished for direct communication. Many times Margaret had been tempted to write a letter to her daughter and enclose it with Aggie's, but she never had.

All that before "it" happened and his incapacitating stroke had suddenly freed her of the fear of Hugh. At one time that dreadful emotion had turned her into a trembling jelly, and she suspected he would know if she'd ever written. Helpless as he now was, he still glared at her belligerently whenever she entered his rooms. In fact she had taken to avoiding a visit completely on the days she received a letter.

The name *Bruce MacAlister* lingered in Rosie's mind, too, as she pummeled the weekly wash, taking her back to the one time before when he'd been mentioned in the papers. The bell broke through her thoughts, and Rosie sighed, drying her hands quickly. She'd never get the washing done at this rate. A good job the linens from the old man's bed were done separately by his own attendants. She hoped Mistress Munro wouldn't keep her too long, because the one called Alec would soon be in for his daily cup of tea.

Even in his extremity nothing softened Hugh Munro. Unable to express his terrible anger within, except for the cold hate exuding from his eyes, he seethed with memories, especially the ones of that night two years ago, when his living had ceased and this existence had begun.

Making his way home on the public tram, he had struggled to keep the mounting fury from showing through his facade of cold composure. From the moment in the morning when his new clerk had underlined an article in the *Times* for his attention and he had scanned it before realizing the implications, this fury had been on him. For the remainder of the day he had avoided his colleagues, but the other lawyers serving in the council chambers had all learned from his bitter insults in the past not to broach him when the customary scowl darkened his face.

Searching for something else to discuss had been no better. It had seemed the only subject being brought before the chambers these days all concerned the highlands. Cases of crofters daring to protest against their lairds, who had seized grazing land for grouse shooting, after the tenants had paid their year's rent, had filled Hugh's portfolio. Normally these cases had not reached his desk. The highlanders, always squabbling among themselves, usually settled that way, too, but times had begun to change, and Hugh Munro hated change. Had he been given foresight of the drastic change that day would bring to his own life, he would have taken steps to have finished it while he had control. As it was, unless a matter had his prior approval, he would not tolerate change.

He writhed now in his prison of a bed as he noted the man Alec slipping out the door for the usual consorting with the maid. Oh, what he would do to those two when he regained his faculties. His mind strayed again to the last day when he had been able to walk. Entering his own front door, everything had appeared as usual, until he had stepped into his study. There the unprecedented sight of Margaret calmly usurping his place in front of the fire had caused his pent-up fury to surface. In all their forty-five years of marriage, such a thing had never happened before. Very early in their life together his patterns had been established. Attempting to somehow keep his dignity while showing his infinite displeasure, he had stood for a full minute by the clock, unable to calculate what this could be about. Margaret had known his study to be sacrosanct and never entered there. What was this? Should he ignore her? She had not allowed him to ignore her. The worm had turned. It was then he heard the incredible statement.

"Hugh, I'm going to see Elspeth. She is our only child, and we've denied her long enough. I want some money!"

"Margaret, you know better than even to be in here. Besides all else, your strength. . . ." He knew that, if she allowed him to keep talking, his iron will and his ability to twist words would undo her. But worse was to follow as she broke in on his diatribe.

"My strength is fine." His snort of laughter turned to a screech of derision, and a violent trembling began in his limbs as he recalled the article in the *Times*. That was when something had exploded within his head, and he had picked up the poker!

Margaret's voice had risen to a scream: "No, Hugh. You wouldn't?"

"Shut your mouth!" This was always the place where his mind refused to remember, because those were the last words he had uttered to this day.

His eyes swiveled to the door as he heard it open. That upstart Alec had not stayed so long in the kitchen today. But it was not Alec who appeared in his restricted line of vision. It was Margaret. Something different shone from her despised face.

In the kitchen Rosie was recounting her version of the news item and telling how it reminded her of the other time Reverend Bruce MacAlister's name had been in the papers. But Alec had heard all that before. He was more interested in the teller, and she had once again to slap his hand as he tried to pull her into an embrace. How many times did she have to tell him she was a decent Catholic girl and did not allow any such liberties?

A loud scream, followed by a crash, propelled both of them out the door and along the corridor to the sickroom. An unbelievable sight met their eyes. Spread-eagle on the carpet in front of his bed couch lay the great lawyer! He who had not been able to move without strong men lifting him for more than two years! Standing over him, trembling in every limb, stood Margaret Munro, brandishing a massive fire iron.

12

Rosie's immediate thought, *Serves him right, the cantankerous old sod. I hope she did a good job*, was immediately replaced with, *This canna be!*

Margaret stood staring dully at the fire iron in her hand.

"Sweet Jesus! Mistress Munro, what have you done?"

"He's not dead, Rosie."

She called me Rosie without being reminded of it.

"I did nothing but hold this up to defend myself when he lunged at me. After all, he hasn't moved since. . . . He just fell over. Dear God! Where is his attendant?"

Alec, who had been standing behind Rosie, with mouth agape at this appalling sight, moved in to reclaim his authority. "I'm here! We heard all the commotion and came at once. Let me see if he's alive. Send for the doctor, mistress."

"Rosie, will you send Jimmy for Dr. Chisholm?"

It took four men to get Hugh Munro off the floor and back onto the bed.

Doctor Chisholm shook his head. "This is beyond my knowledge. He sat up and grasped your throat, Mistress Munro? He should never have had the strength!"

Margaret's dignity came to the fore. "I'm not accustomed to telling lies, doctor. Your amazement is nothing compared to my own."

"I'm sorry, mistress, but well, anyway, from now on he must

never be left without an attendant. This surge of strength was momentary, I believe, but we canna risk it. Maybe we should be putting him away."

Margaret interrupted again. "No, no. Another attendant, yes—even two more. But no Bedlam. I don't think this will ever happen again. He knows what we're saying, and I'd never sleep another wink if we put him away."

Some days later Margaret again stood beside the improvised daybed. She had asked the doctor to hold nothing back, and he had not. Gazing down at Hugh, she felt only compassion—not for the man lying there, but for what he might have been. Dr. Chisholm had explained that Hugh was not really any worse for the episode and that, very likely, he was as aware as ever of everything being said and done.

With no notion of gloating, she spoke very deliberately and clearly. "Hugh, you heard what Dr. Chisholm said about straining to move. If you attempt it again, it will more than likely kill you. Now that may not bother you as much as this will. He has ordered you to be restrained more severely if you try to hurt me or anyone else again. I think deep down you still want to live, even in this condition, thereby keeping us at your beck and call as we've been for many years. However we have the ability to send you away. Nobody wants that, least of all yourself." His eyes were shut, but she knew he would be following every word.

"We have ordered a bed on wheels for you, and Mister Peddie, the carpenter, is coming next week to change the windows in your study into French windows. Then you can be wheeled outside on nice days. Two more male nurses, in addition to Alec, will care for all your daily requirements and even anticipate them." She glanced over to where one of the new attendants had already set up a corner table holding a book or two and, she noted with a shudder, a set of police handcuffs in full view.

"The doctor has a plan for you to be able to communicate

more. He will explain it to your attendants, and they will teach it to you."

Steeling herself to look at his face again, she noted how the muscles down and to the left side had forged a new set of folds, making him more than ever a caricature of the handsome man he used to be. His eyes had not changed though. He condescended to open them at that moment. Purest hate flowed out of them directly to her. Close to a lifetime of habit caused her to falter briefly, but then she stiffened her resolve and continued, "These are my plans, Hugh. First I will try to visit our Elspeth again. I'll remind you that Elspeth's first husband was an illegitimate son of the Highland chieftain of the ClanRanald. But his surrogate father was named MacAlister."

At the sound of the hated name, the black eyes flashed a spurt of venom and what might have passed for a groan escaped the gray, foam-flecked, lips. Some saliva slopped out, and Margaret calmly leaned over to wipe it away.

"From your law practice you are aware that these chieftains never leave their offspring, legitimate or otherwise, in any lack. As I was saying, after I visit Elspeth, who is comfortable and happy enough, I will find our grandson, Bruce. A new controversy surrounds him at the moment, and I will find out if he requires assistance of any kind. He's proud, like you, Hugh, and I have tried to help him before, but he has refused me. According to that newspaper story, he's venturing out on a kind of itinerant evangelical crusade, independent of denomination. I will try again to make him accept a sizable donation for his work! This time I'll remind him, as I do you at this moment, of the many years of missing Christmas and birthday presents, as well as a wedding present, to make up to him. This is what I came to tell you the other morning when you took the second spell." Margaret paused for breath, and her eyes filled. "Bruce has recently been widowed, you know!"

She sighed. He must hear everything. Glad that he had once again closed his eyes, she went on, "Our great-granddaughter, Mary Jean, is two years old, and I want to see her again. I don't suppose we will live to see her grow up, Hugh, but we are rich people, rich enough to settle an annuity upon her, and so I will instruct our lawyer to put that in the will at once. I've hardly used the power of attorney granted when you first became incompetent." She stopped speaking to watch for a possible reaction to this, but nothing stirred.

"As for you and dying, Hugh, Dr. Chisholm assures me you could live for many more years with very little change, but the chances of your ever seeing Mary are slight, although you never know."

A glance at the clock showed that her "little talk" to her husband had lasted half an hour. She had said more to him in that short time than she had said in a quarter of a century. A discreet knock on the door announced the arrival of Dr. Chisholm. Rosie served tea and left them. If Mistress Munro was above gloating about the turn events had taken, the maid was not. Rosie could still hardly believe it. Old Mistress Munro was getting stronger every day, to be sure, but who would ever have thought she had it in her? Another journey to Skye and thon farm but, after that, to London Town, and she, Rosie Ballantyne, would be going, too.

13

Sleep evaded Dr. Peter Blair. Reaching over to pick up his watch, a turnip of a timepiece that had been his father's gift to mark his emancipation into the sacred brotherhood of medicine, he groaned. Only ten minutes since he had last noted the hour to be the useless one of three o'clock in the morning. Neither day nor night. Through his mind hammered the conversation between George Bennett and himself as the carriage clip-clopped through the midnight streets a mere three hours ago. George had started it.

"Now do you see what I mean about God's providence for the MacAlister?"

"Not at all, sir. Quite the contrary in fact. Would you have me believe that your God, to bring the 'apple of his eye,' as you called Bruce, into line, allowed him to be bereaved and then almost go mad with the grief of it? The cruelest of human fathers, or the pettiest, would hardly stoop to that." In the dim interior Peter had felt the loving concern emanating from this man he now called friend.

The reply was gentle. "Peter, you remind me so much of Charles when we were both starry-eyed idealists. He, in his zeal, declared if man would show more humanity to his fellows, the Utopia would come. I, tottering high on some form of holy pedestal, declared only God could do it in His sovereign will and time. I still believe that, of course, but I know now that

God's way is balanced. It includes the application of what Charles declares, and I—"

"Sorry, sir, but I am not in the mood for your fond memories. What does all that have to do with our highland laddie getting ready to challenge the sins of all Scotland, beginning with his own kirk? Why, during our student days at Granny Mac's, to be 'ordained' was considered the crowning achievement of his life and marrying Bonnie Jean a close second. Now he has lost both, and you want me to believe God, if there is a God, is doing the MacAlister a good turn? I'll not have any dealings with that kind of God, thank you."

The carriage stopped as he finished speaking, and the driver prepared for the usual long wait. These two could talk the shoes off a highlandman when they started the debating. Almost immediately, however, the young doctor jumped down, slamming the door.

George called out, "I do understand, Peter. Keep your mind open, but leave the questions be for the time being. We'll expect you next Friday as usual."

It was the phrase "keep your mind open" that echoed and reechoed in Peter's head.

That phrase, or one very similar, had been Agatha Rose's parting words to him on the day he arrived back in Glasgow, after Jean's funeral. Since then he had been trying with all his willpower to do the opposite, filling his life with work from early morning till late night, never refusing a sick call, whatever the hour. Another irony on this night of sleeplessness was that the bell, often ringing unceasingly, had remained silent since he lay down. Rare indeed!

Giving up on sleep, he allowed the seed thought of Agatha Rose to take root. Her theme song was not unlike George's—or Bruce's, either. Variations of the same theme, in fact. But for all her delicate ways, Agatha's rejection of his proposal had been blunt. He had lured her, confident in himself that she would say yes to his question, to the summerhouse at Strathcona

House. Instead of the joyful acceptance he had anticipated, he had received a cool calculated no that had amazed him.

"There are two reasons, Peter. The first one is that I would need to be fully convinced that you are a true Christian. I could not be yoked to an unbeliever. I know we have courted, and I've led you to believe. . . . At first I was filled with romantic ideas like we were meant for each other, as Jean and Bruce were, and the Lord would bring a solution. Now I see how that was thinking like a child. You must be truly 'born again' before I could consider marrying you. I think you've just been pretending, to please me." He started to protest, but she waved two fingers at him.

"The second thing may make you change your mind anyway. I don't want to have babies, since coming home from Skye and praying about what happened to Jean. Oh, I've heard the talk, as you and the other men discussed overpopulation and such, so I'll be going home to Yorkshire for a while and then back to the mission in London. Later on I'll likely be sailing for India or maybe Africa. They haven't said what place yet, but as Auntie Faye's in India, maybe I'll ask for Calcutta." Words had failed Peter. No more had been said, and they had parted with a formal handshake at the door of the house. The next day George Bennett had showed him a short note, hand delivered by messenger: "Dear Uncle George: I'm going on the night train. I ask for your prayers and blessing. Please inform Dr. Peter. A.R.G."

Peter had read the note and handed it back in silence. The subject had been closed.

Wishing that he could close the matter now and get some sleep, Peter turned onto his other side. On Saturday, which was today already, he'd planned to write some more of his notes on reform. Why not get up and start now? Peter crawled out of the bed covers, but instead of the notes, he found himself writing a letter: "My dear highland laddie. . . . "

"My dear highland laddie . . . ," Bruce smiled at the silly title before reading on:

Having just read in the *Times* of your latest escapade and having some of it confirmed by Granny Mac herself, at Strathcona House, it seems to me, lad, that you are in dire need of some solid, earthbound counsel. Here it comes for nothing. Give up this delusion of saving the world, before they crucify you! There is a place for you here in Glasgow. Yes, I know you worked in the Gorbals before and felt it was not really your calling, but we got on so well together during your curateship and achieved some good things.

Mary Jean would be well cared for at Granny Mac's (the dragon would be delirious with joy at the idea) while you joined me in my work here in the slums. We could pick up where you left off. I'm no fatalist, as you know, and I think men have the capabilities to change their own circumstances. Charles Booth (I know you and he don't get on too well) has some good things to say on that score. He is a pioneer in rousing folk to help themselves, and even you can't help admiring that in a person. I do—admire him, I mean. If you could read some of the reports passing through the clinic here—reports on atrocities being carried out in your dear highlands and isles, not only sanctioned by your "kirk" but being blessed by some of your collar-turned-round hypocrites, and all in the name of Christ. Now I know you and George Bennett and a few others deplore these things, but still they're happening. My friend *wipe the dust of that kirk off your feet forever.* The truth is *they do not deserve you, laddie.* Besides I need you here!

This letter is too long, but I have more to say. In spite of the foregoing, I think I might be having a change of heart in my own self, maybe even the first birth pangs leading up to what young Agatha Rose Gordon calls being "born again." By the by did you know she has scorned my humble proposal? That sounds soppy, so I'll say no more on the subject for the present. Meanwhile consider well what I said about Glasgow. I mean it. Don't bother to answer, just come.

Yours truly,
Peter Blair, M.D.

P.S.: If you've really got a caravan, leave it at the farm in Aribaig. We'll tour the inland locks next summer. Eh? P.B

P.S.S.: Don't say a word to anybody about what I said about a change of heart. I still have a lot of ???????s. Your Jesus is all right, but your kirk, no thank you. P.B."

"Get thee behind me with your temptations, Peter, boy." Thinking he was alone in the manse kitchen, Bruce spoke his thoughts aloud after reading the long letter.

"Are ye talkin' to me?" Hamish stood behind his chair, and Bruce glanced up.

"Och, no, Hamish, just thinking out loud. Did you want something?"

"Aye. Ye've got visitors. They must've come off the mail boat, I think."

"Well, where are they now? Did you tell them?" Bruce and Hamish had a working arrangement to deal with the curious, who still came seeking tales of the sensational miracle. Hamish would give his version of what happened, and often enough this would satisfy. Some people asked him to pray over beads or hankies, but Hamish balked at that. Bruce would be called then, and after reading a bit from the Bible, he would pray as requested.

"They're no' asking aboot the meeracle. The auld yin is yer granny, and she wants to talk to you."

14

Bruce's brow cleared as he rushed toward the door. Painful memories still surrounded his mother's maiden name, but he knew no harm resided within his much-persecuted grandmother.

"Grandmother! It is you. Hamish, put on the tea!" But Hamish had already gone into the kitchen for that purpose. "Come into the parlor and sit here."

He pushed Peter's letter into a drawer, wondering if he should bother with the looking glass. His habit of twisting a strand of hair round and round in his fingers usually left him resembling a woolly sheep dragged through a hedge backward, as his mother would say. Patting it absently, he decided he would do fine. Smiling, he faced the old lady.

Rosie waited, wondering what she should do now, until Hamish came in with the tea tray. This was behavior she understood, so she helped him with the serving.

Hamish whispered, "Would you be wantin' to see Mary Jean? She's at the farm, but it's no' far to walk."

The maid glanced at her mistress, who nodded. "On you go, Aggie."

Rosie sighed. Wrong name again, but she said nothing, and the two left together. Margaret Munro turned to Bruce.

The name *Aggie* had set the memories stirring in Bruce, and he began to recall, vaguely at first, he and his mother running along a dark lane. It was raining, and his mother did not stop to let him put on his cap and jacket. Then suddenly they were inside a warm place filled with men. The room smelled funny, and the men spoke roughly, but the feeling of being safe had engulfed him. "The Crossroads Inn."

"I beg your pardon, Bruce, but did you say 'the Crossroads Inn' "?

"Yes, when you said 'Aggie,' a memory stirred, and the inn's name came to mind. I don't know why!"

"I think I know why, Bruce. The first time we saw each other you were a little lad of scarcely four years old. It will ever be a source of terrible regret to me that I waited so long to find you again, but to return to that time. Your mother sought refuge at the inn you named just now, when my husband offended her beyond endurance. I take it she never explained any of that to you?" Bruce shook his head, and she continued. "Then neither will I. Suffice to say it's all water under the bridge, and conditions have altered considerably."

"Is my grandfather dead then?" Tensely Bruce awaited her answer, his voice almost a whisper.

"No. His condition is unchanged since I saw you last." They sat silently for a time.

"I received a picture postcard from Mam the other day, saying she and Andrew would be away on a holiday. A real holiday, mind you! Not just an excursion for a day or two, but for a whole month. An unheard-of occurrence. The card was posted in London! Who knows where the next stop will be?"

"Yes, I know about that. Aggie and I—oh, dear I really must stop calling her Aggie; she's my young traveling companion—have just come from the farm in Aribaig, and we heard all about the proposed journey from your esteemed grandfather and namesake when he was giving us instructions about the new ferry across to Skye. I admit to some surprise at your mother's jaunting, but I am discovering how life itself can be most surprising."

"Life or people or both?"

Margaret opened her handbag and removed a folded newspaper clipping. She smoothed it carefully, with long, white fingers, before replying, "I realize I have no right to ask, but could you humor a weak, frustrated old lady, by telling her what has been happening to you in recent weeks? Your mother wrote, telling me of your loss, and I'm so sorry. You see, I became fully wrapped up in self-pity again, and— Oh, I must not make excuses." Diving into the bag again, she pulled out a dainty white hankie and began to dab at her eyes. "Oh, I'm cross with myself. I have been sad enough all these years."

"Don't be cross, Grandmother, and don't worry if you cry. Mother always cries most when she's happy, anyway. Of course I'll tell you." Bruce crossed the room and took up the small hand nervously clutching the paper. He pressed it to his lips. At once the few tears became a flood, and Bruce held her close until the storm of weeping subsided. Not until she composed herself did he begin to relate his story.

". . . So there are those who sit in high places and consider that I have stepped out of bounds because I will not concede, even after this time lapse, that our escape from the sea was less than a miracle. Others desired to make more of it by turning us into a sideshow, but that was not my doing. I merely wanted to give God the glory and continue my ministry. That's what I've tried to do until my—until Jean. . . ." Margaret moved at that moment to ease a cramped arm, and to cover his still-too-raw emotion, Bruce went to fetch her another cushion.

"Could you not have done that quietly, then, without upsetting the elders and rulers?" she questioned.

"Seemingly not and be honest. But it's all the same now. When you've been as close to death as Hamish and I, you change your mind about values, and now with Jean gone, suddenly I've not so much to lose any more. In a way I'd been blind, but now I'm starting to see."

"What is it you see, Bruce?"

"I see, through a glass darkly at the moment, but I do perceive how, down through the ages, God's truth has been twisted and warped by men. From Adam and Eve in the garden to those who listened to Moses give the Law without wanting to hear it or, if they heard, not applying it. Even some of those who walked with the Lord Himself missed the point!"

"Is there no hope for us, then?"

"Of course there's hope. God knew who would and who would not hear and respond. He always had a man or woman to take up the torch. It flickered, close to going out many times, when some of those privileged to carry it were in danger. Even today, in our so-called Christian land, it is under a bushel of pious-sounding apathy. But it will never be allowed to go out."

"Do you say then you are one of those torch bearers?"

"I do. Without false modesty, but humble before God at being chosen, I do say so! I pray for strength of body and mind as well as the ability to submit to the Holy Spirit for His power to go to the end."

"You could be crucified, you know? In fact I think you are already on the whipping stand before Pilate." Margaret had eased slightly away from Bruce so that she could see him better.

"Grandmother, I perceive you as a poet-prophet. You remind me of my friend Peter, Dr. Peter Blair, to be correct, whose letter I just finished reading before you arrived today. He says the same thing about my being crucified. I hesitate to remind you of the Scripture verse 'I am crucified with Christ, nevertheless. . . .' I'm sure you are familiar with it. Here, read Peter's letter for yourself while I see where Hamish has got to. I thought he went to fetch Mary from the Gould farm. Elliott and his good wife took her for a while so that we could finish the packing up. We're flitting tomorrow, you know? Everything is in the crates already and Hamish . . . I wonder? Hamish!"

Hamish heard the shout as he walked up the path. Not wide enough to be called a street and too wide for a lane, with rhododendrons on either side and touching overhead, the path was a pleasant place to walk in. Rosie walked in front of him, holding Mary Jean by the hand. She had just asked him how such bonnie bushes grew so well in such a wildlike place.

Before he could answer, he heard Bruce's call. He carried a bundle containing the farewell gifts presented by a frankly weeping Mistress Gould. Placing it on the doorstep, he hurried inside, leaving Rosie chattering busily to a wide-eyed Mary Jean.

"I've helped to rear my wee brothers and sisters since I was a bairn myself. My, you're a bonnie wee lass. My mistress will be pleased."

Rosie had learned much from the suddenly talkative Mistress Munro, on their train journey north. This very obliging fellow, running ahead of her up the walk where the path widened, had filled in the other gaps in the story. She was still unsure where he fitted in. Was he a servant, or did he mean it when he called thon handsome minister his brother? Some churches called everybody brother or sister, she knew, and maybe that's what he meant. Giving up trying to sort out who was who, Rosie decided to ask him—Hamish Cormack was his name—later on.

Margaret Munro's greeting of her great-granddaughter was ecstatic. Mary Jean took it as her due at first but quickly turned to Hamish for enlightenment. He in turn left the explanations to Bruce.

"This is another Granny for you, love. We'll call her Granny Munro." But the word was too much for Mary to master, so her newest grandmother became forever "Granny Munny." Rosie thought this a great joke, but she kept her glee to share with the family when she got home. Her daddy would like that one. Rosie got a further surprise when she discovered yet another side to Mistress Munro, one she had never before suspected. That lady had completely taken charge of the domestic situation.

"Don't look so shocked, Rosie. Of course I can cook. When Hamish brings the meat and vegetables, I'll show you. You can help by getting everything ready for the table. We'll need to open some of those crates, and I'm glad someone had the foresight to mark what was in them. Mind you, the fish crates have their distinct odor, but that won't matter. This'll be just like the picnics we used to go on before. Oh, here's Hamish!"

"Johnny MacVie was chust in wi' his boat, loaded wi' herrin' as fresh as. . . . Ah, aye, well, I have this oatmeal and some o' thae tatties left in yon bag and. . . ."

"Enough said, Hamish. This night we'll feast in better style than Queen Victoria herself at Balmoral. There's eggs and brown sugar for a caramel custard, and we'll whip up some of that cream with a fork. Rosie, you can do that. Even Mary Jean can help. At her age now it's time she started anyway." Rosie marveled some more. Mistress Munro looked and sounded like a new woman—a woman twenty years younger, going on a new lease on life. The handsome minister was laughing at her antics, shaking his head at the same time, but he was pleased, too, she could tell. As for that Hamish, a pity he wasn't ten years younger. *Dinna be silly, Rosie!* she admonished herself as she bent to the tasks at hand. *Take each blessing as it comes, as Daddy always says.* As another of her daddy's sayings came to mind, she spoke it aloud: "Time will tell!"

Rosie's daddy, a philosopher in his own environment, had always taught her that to look further forward than the day you were in was asking for trouble, and if people could see what really waited ahead for them, they could not face it most of the time.

The meal, crisply fried herring, alongside a potato baked in the hot coals, and garnished with the curly shoots of dandelion leaves mixed into a tasty salad dish, was quickly demolished. The promised custard had curdled, but no one complained. The sweet morsel slid down to refresh the palate and leave the mouth tingling.

Tingling was all that remained of the feast as Margaret and Bruce talked well into the night. Mary Jean slept in her cot by the fire, having been bathed and admired in turn by both women. Hamish was off somewhere, repacking the crates, and Rosie dozed on the rocking chair.

Bruce opened his heart to his grandmother. He told her about

Jean, and at last he was able to speak of that terrible morning when he lost her. At that point his grandmother held out her arms, and he went and knelt at her feet. After a while he began to tell her about the happy years at the croft, with Gran'pa Bruce and his mother and Andrew. He told her, too, about his university days and about his special friends. Peter Blair and George Bennett, Faye Felicity and Granny MacIntyre and Raju. He even told her about that long-ago day when he delivered the knock-out punch to Jean's father, and when Margaret smiled, he shook his head at her.

"It was not amusing, Grandmother. The Word says we are to honor parents and those in authority. I broke that law."

"Bruce, you force me to remind you of First John one, nine, for I sense you've applied it at other times. 'He is faithful and just to forgive us. . . .' "

"Yes, I have applied it many times. I could not live with my guilt otherwise."

They sat then for some time in companionable silence. All the sounds of the household had settled into nighttime shufflings, with Rosie's snoring a tiny murmur in the stillness. Hamish had slipped away to his place in the attic.

Finally Bruce spoke, his voice a whisper. "Could you tell me about my father, Grandmother? Mam would never speak about him, and the bare facts, that he was a good man in spite of what I might hear or guess to the contrary, was all I ever got from Gran'pa Bruce or Fraser."

"Yes, Bruce, I'll agree he was a good man. I believe that now, but I did not always think so. For many years I held a grudge, blaming him for devastating our family life. But I see where Hugh, my husband, your other grandfather, has this terrible barrier against any kind of love. He considers it to be a form of weakness.

"I can only relate this from our point of view. Elspeth was the apple of her father's eye as far as he was able to go. He never told her that, of course, but we knew. Hugh didn't seem the least bit concerned that we had no son. Desiring to be different from his colleagues, he took Elspeth into the law business the day after she finished at the academy for young ladies. She had passed all her exams with flying colors. The university would not admit women, so he determined to train Elspeth himself. We planned a celebration for her twentieth birthday. She'd been working along with her father for the three years between, and her coming out as a legal scribe was to be a red-letter day. Hugh's staff and his colleagues at the bar were to be shown what his girl could do. They, Elspeth and her father, traveled together to his private chambers every day. Inevitably she met the other scribes and students of the law. John Keir MacAlister was one of them. Did your mother ever tell you how much you resemble him?"

"No, never! But Gran'pa Bruce might have mentioned it! Do I, indeed?"

"You do, although I see a family likeness to my husband as well. Now, for instance, as you knit your brows together in puzzlement. In fact, as truly as two men hated each other—and I'm afraid it was mutual, Bruce, because of your mother—they were strangely similar in many ways. But John suffered! Oh, how he suffered for humanity." Her own suffering brought a sigh from deep within, and Bruce waited.

"Before we realized what was happening between our daughter and John MacAlister, my husband had brought some of the senior students to our house for a debate. Your father won, hands down. John could silver tongue his way through a mob of orators! Hugh should have guessed something was in the air, but he did not. When my husband and I at last realized nothing would stop this upstart crofter's son from marrying our daughter, we were too late. Hugh not only cut her out of his life, but he began at once to use every bit of influence, even bribery, to ensure that your father would never become a lawyer, at least not in Scotland. John gave up with very little struggle and returned to the croft with your mother. You know the rest."

Softly, Bruce said, "No, I don't know the rest. Not all of it. I believe my mother had a conspiracy of secrecy. I never learned how he died."

"He was a good man, Bruce, but a weak one. You resemble him in appearance, but you seem to have inherited his most admirable attributes and escaped the others. You have a strong will, like my husband, tempered with that ingrained goodness from John. You have the same kind of sensitivity your father suffered from, but I believe it is balanced by some solid reasoning power, again from your grandfather Munro. God has a work for you, and He has combined all this into yourself. You will fulfill that purpose!" She stopped again, and now she yawned politely. "I am very tired, Bruce. I must ask you to excuse me."

"I'm sorry, but not yet, Grandmother. You say I have a work to do for God, and I know that already. My calling is clear and plain. You are present here as part of that purpose, so God will renew your strength as we wait upon Him. I feel I must learn all there is about my father's death before I can embark on the kind of ministry opening up to me now. If there is some dark shadow, I should be aware of it."

"Yes, you are right. I must tell you all I know, although I warn you I only know what your mother chose to tell me that day long ago. Never fear, I do not consider this story to be sinister. Full of tragedy and irony, perhaps, and scattered with if onlys, but not sinister. John MacAlister could not change the world or the people in it, so he had a wish to die. This is more common than we imagine. Many do not want to continue to face life. I have felt that myself many times, but I took the road of least resistance. Your father tried to escape through drinking spirits." She lifted her eyes at that, to see his reaction, but he was staring off into space, so she went on.

"Elspeth told me, that one and only time I've seen her since she left home, how she could never understand. She had thought when they were married that he would settle down to wedded bliss and their love would be enough. As for earning a living, his natural father had insured he would always be provided for, but his ambitions as a lawyer and orator had been crushed, and he could never settle to farm life. After you were born, your mother became engrossed in you for a time—a natural occurrence for new mothers with their firstborn. One day, she told me it was one of those highland days when the sun never shines through the black clouds, she peeped into the room where you were supposed to be sleeping. Your father stood at the open window, holding you high and giving you an exposé of the sad state of the world. She ran in and snatched you from him, quickly finding out he was intoxicated to the point of stupor. Again as mothers do, she raged at him for a minute, saying things such as that he didn't deserve to be your father. When she turned back from tending you, John had disappeared into the mists. Apparently he walked to the village of Aribaig, took in some more liquid refreshment, and started to walk back. When he failed to return to the croft, your mother and grandfather went looking with lanterns. They found him and carried him home. He developed a bad case of pneumonia and died of it. The verdict was 'exposure while under the influence of alcohol.' I'm sorry, Bruce, I thought you might have known some of this."

Bruce's sigh was long and deep. "No, I was very young at the time, and afterward, well, I don't remember hearing it spoken about at all."

"Your mother never doubted you would be a minister. She assured me of it that day she brought you to see me. I wonder if your father would have approved or sanctioned it?"

"My mother's plan for me happened to be part of God's purpose for my life. About what might have been, had my father lived, who knows? The Bible says, 'God's ways are not our ways,' and further 'His ways are past finding out.' I take that to mean not to pry too deeply or even try to find out. Take it all in faith. Someday, and in a twinkling, we will be given closer understanding."

"Bruce, I'm nearly sixty-five years old, and this day has been one of my happiest. You are all and more any grandmother could wish for. No longer will I complain about my life, since God has allowed me this day. Much of my trouble was of my own making, so I'll just say this and be done with it. When I married my man, I saw in his strength only good, and I turned my mind away from the other side of his nature. I think my daughter did the same in a different way. She saw in her John's softness what she wanted to see, and she took on the impossible job of reforming him. The age-old story." Margaret sighed with a true weariness, and this time Bruce had pity.

"Grandmother, indeed and you are very tired. Slip into my bed now. Hamish took a message to Jamieson MacRae not to bring the cart for the flitting until time for the later boat, so sleep in as long as you want."

"Let me finish saying this first. I see in you a mixture of what was good in Hugh Munro and John MacAlister as well as some added bits from some of the rest of us. God has made you yourself. God bless you, my dear one. Forgive an old lady her few maudlin moments and tears. Now, where is Aggie—I mean Rosie?" At her name Rosie emerged from the depths of the giant rocking chair and, without a word, led her mistress through the doorway.

·ᘍ 15 ᘓ·

When Hamish arrived at Jamieson MacRae's door, next morning, the two hardly needed words.

"You'll no' be wantin' the cart the day yet?" was Jamieson's greeting. As Hamish nodded, the other man continued, "We would be pleased if ye never needed it. He's bound and determined to go, though?" The villagers were used to the sight of visitors at the manse, so as no further remarks were required, Hamish returned to his duties. A good breakfast his minister brother would have after spending the night praying and even now being away up on the moors.

When Bruce announced his intention to delay the "flitting" for one more day, no one at the breakfast table seemed surprised. The meal had progressed in much the same way as the supper the night before. Rosie's initial unease soon left as she realized the changes in her mistress were still evident. There was a limit though, and when Bruce began with the big words again, Hamish and Rosie slipped away to the kitchen. Somebody still had to do the cleaning-up jobs.

"Dredging up the past is not expedient unless it produces better actions now." Margaret and Bruce still sat at the table, but the conversation merely took up where they had left it off the night before. "The Bible says forgetting those things which are behind, we must press on toward the mark which is the prize of the high calling of God. So today we must concern ourselves mainly with the present and, to a lesser degree, the future."

Margaret nodded wisely before replying, "Yes, Bruce. May I be allowed a small part in all this?" His brows furrowed into their pensive groove, and he seemed to withdraw for a while. Sensing her grandson was communing with God, Margaret settled to wait quietly. Sipping her tea, she examined the fragile cup Hamish had produced with a proprietary flourish from one of the fish crates the previous night. The set of dishes, as Jean had explained to Hamish and Hamish had passed on to the attentive audience, was "a fine heirloom tea set from the MacIntyre family, part of Mistress Jean's dowry!" The fancy words meant little to Hamish, but the fragile dishes, so incongruous in his rough fingers, were treated with tender loving care.

Margaret's thoughts returned to her present surroundings. Bruce still seemed far away. Since Elspeth's marriage and consequent move to the highlands, her original ideas about the wilds of Scotland had undergone frequent changes. Nothing had prepared her for the truth. The few inns in which she and Rosie had lodged in recent days had proven much less primitive than she had imagined. Still, some of the scenery did show strange old stone houses and even some grass-walled dwellings that didn't appear to have any chimneys or windows. The result of these contrasts left her not knowing what to expect from Aribaig. The reality of the amenities at the croft had delighted her: the pantiled roof and glass windows and, inside, the modern range with its large oven, close by the stone sink with running water and— wonder of wonders—a bathroom as well equipped as the one in her own house in Edinburgh. Here in the manse, the facilities, although not as modern, were entirely adequate. Bruce's voice recalled her attention to the present and her request.

"Grandmother, in what way do you mean you want a part in all this?"

"Obviously I cannot go with you on your missionary journeys, and I can see you are determined to 'go into all the world,' so to speak. Last time I was here, you refused a gift, but I, well,

I hoped that maybe this time—Oh, Bruce, please allow me to make a financial contribution to your work."

"Do you have your husband's permission to offer this?"

"Not exactly. He is unable to make decisions at present, so I—"

"No! Without your husband's consent I cannot accept your offer. I'm sorry, Grandmother, but that is God's way. If I took help from you, even your well-intentioned kindness, detecting as I do questionable motives and a wrong source, the work cannot be blessed." Margaret began to weep, and he walked round the table to her side. The sobs subsided while he held her hand.

"You are quite right, Bruce. Part of my reason for helping you came from knowing that Hugh would hate it. Revenge! After all the years of being less than a doormat, at least he noticed and wiped his feet on them. I suddenly find myself able to do whatever I please. My first reaction was to take all I felt I had a right to. This knowledge went to my head. But you, so young and so wise, have shown me that without responsibilities I have no rights. All my life I have avoided responsibility. My plans were that after settling some money with you, I would go with Rosie to London for the winter, but now I am uncertain again."

Bruce, listening gravely, with his head to the side, had no such uncertainties. "You must return to Edinburgh. Your husband needs you! Tell him you forgive him for all the wrongs, and then tend him as long as he needs tending."

Margaret gasped. "But he is well attended. Now more than ever. He doesn't need me."

"I believe he needs you more than he ever has before. You may never hear him say so, but still—"

"Yes! You're right again, Bruce." She gave him a tearful smile. "I've avoided him as if he had the plague and not just since his stroke, either. I think I'm relieved. I've missed my own bed and my house. I'll go home and try harder to reach Hugh." Again the smile, so like his mother's, flashed, and she said coyly, "You will allow me to give wee Mary a present, won't you?"

He smiled back but was still cautious. "That all depends."

"Oh, it's not money, although I'm going to say this and then leave the subject. Hugh and I have accumulated a lot of money. More than half of it is mine, from my own father's estate, and as your mother is our only child, she will inherit everything, according to Scottish law. Hugh, I discovered from his advocate after his accident, has never bothered to make a will. Like doctors and even preachers, I believe, lawyers tend not to practice what they tell others to do. Being Hugh, he likely thought no one, not even God Himself, would dare to take his life from him. When the time comes, I rely on you to help persuade your mother to accept this money. Elspeth's attempt at reconciliation, though futile, entitles her to this. Subsequently it will all be yours. By then, God willing, you will feel free to take it as God's provision and use it to further His Kingdom. For this day then let me have my moment of the joy of giving to my great-grandchild." Searching his face closely, she was reassured by the smile. "Rosie! Rosie, bring the hamper."

Hamish it was who brought in the hamper and waited for the unveiling. A treasure trove of clothes and toys emerged from the hastily unearthed box. The pièce de résistance was last to come forth: a robe of the softest and most exquisite chinchilla fur. It could be spread out for a bed cover or folded double and fastened with snaps to form a cozy bag. Margaret and Rosie spent a delirious hour with Mary, trying on clothes and showing Hamish and Bruce how each article could be used to best advantage, in the caravan or anywhere.

Bruce and Hamish slipped away to make the belated plans for the move. This had to be the final off-putting, as Hamish would say. The new minister would be arriving the next day. So by the time the glorious sun began to sink into the western ocean, the villagers of Inverechny, parishioners of the wee kirk, for the most part, at last had their chance to bid a fitting farewell to this preacher who had brought such joyous infamy to their village. Agreeing with him or not, most of the businesses had profited in some way by the miracles and supposed resurrections, and all, even the Johnstones, had to admit Reverend

MacAlister was no ordinary minister. So they would have a "ceiliaedh" for him. No whiskey, to be sure, but a song and dance with plenty of shortbread and black buns. Everybody liked a party, and the minister had been sad far too long.

Jamieson had a final word of warning for Hamish, "Watch him from thon Johnstone. He's got it in for him. He'll no give in that easy!"

"But Jamie, that's a' in the past, and he wants to forget it."

"It might be in the past, but it's not forgotten. Siller is a strong reminder of grudges. So chust watch."

"I will then." The two shook hands, and Jamieson turned quickly to hide his feelings.

The party was a memory, and Bruce, not sure how to respond at first, had soon decided that it was meant kindly. He watched the kilted dancers and listened to the pipes and joined in when they sang "Amazing Grace" to the skirl of the pipes. His theory that God would not object to such if a man's heart was right stretched to the limit, but all in all he enjoyed it.

They stood now on the deck of the *Spirit of the Isles*, saying good-bye to Margaret and Rosie. With amazement, they had stood and watched while the great steam crane loaded the caravan at Portree and then unloaded it again on Mallaig's sturdy pier. Margaret was still not sure of its suitability as a dwelling for Bruce and Mary Jean, but she held her peace. The *Spirit* would take her and Rosie to Oban, where they would entrain for Edinburgh. Meanwhile Bruce and Hamish would go to the livery stable in Mallaig. They needed a pair of Clydesdales to pull the caravan home to Aribaig. Bruce's thoughts winged ahead to the days when they would be together on the steading. Home, with his mother and Andrew, Gran'pa Bruce and Hamish, himself and Mary Jean, and maybe even Dugald. Melancholy yapping her head off. What a time they would have, making plans! If he had to turn to wipe a stray tear at the thought of what might have been, no one thought it strange.

16

"**R**osie, my dear, are you disappointed we're not going to London?"

"No, Mistress Munro, as a matter of fact I'm pleased to be goin' home. Two weeks away is long enough for me."

Margaret laughed at her companion, but she had to agree. "I'm missing my own bed and some other things, too. I don't believe I'll be traveling very far again. I think from now on I'll invite my daughter and any others to visit me instead."

They were on the train bound for Edinburgh. Soon they would be chugging into Waverley Station, and the short-lived adventure would be over. The sweet sound of her grandson's heather tones, as he said farewell, echoed softly in Margaret's ear. To be related to such a man was worth all the tribulation she had suffered throughout her life. Even his gentle, but oh, so strong, refusal of money proved again the depth of his character. She, an old lady more than forty years his senior, had learned much from Bruce. Now she could go back to her husband and tell him of this grandson whose very existence Hugh would deny. Even if Hugh never responded to her news, what did it matter? Her words would sink in, as Bruce said, and somehow they would convey truth to this one who shunned all forms of love and turned away from caring of any sort.

Bruce had told her what to do, "Just talk to him, not about me or your life, but about Jesus. Read to him from the Gospel of

John. Read it like a story. You will meet and rediscover the Master in a new way for yourself, Grandmother. When you have read it once or twice through, go on to the Book of Acts and read the first four chapters. Keep repeating them over and over. From there I believe the Holy Spirit will guide you further." He had spoken these words as they waited for the boat to unload the caravan. Hearing Rosie direct the cab driver to Westercrofts Road, Margaret steeled herself. Soon now she would face Hugh, but never again would she fear him—not because he was helpless, but because a man had shown her how to apply the verses she had learned at her own mother's knee. One snippet of a verse kept repeating through her mind as the cab clattered over the cobbles: ". . . perfect love casteth out fear. . . ." Bruce had pointed out how it was not her love that would do this, but God's. All her life she had struggled with having to make her love perfect enough to cast out fear. Now she saw she could never achieve that alone. The sampler on her bedroom wall, over which she had labored for years as a girl, said it best. "God is love!"

The cab driver jumped down to open the door, and Rosie announced the obvious. "We're home, Mistress Munro!"

"So you see, Hugh, I am asking you to forgive me for the unfeeling way I've treated you after your seizures. It was cruel of me. It's a cruel world, Hugh, and we've both given and taken much cruelty." Hugh had closed his eyes after the first flicker of shock, but she knew he heard and understood every word. "I've seen our grandson again, as I told you I would. Somehow I missed seeing Elspeth, but I'm sure there will be other opportunities." The eyes flickered briefly but still he did not look at her. Dr. Chisholm had established a system of communication between him and his attendants, and it consisted simply of a series of eye blinks, one for yes and two for no. What else did he need to say, when you thought about it? Gazing down upon him, Margaret marveled anew that she no longer bore Hugh a grudge. Although he had warped her life, he had warped his own also, and one should feel nothing but pity. Picking up her Bible, Margaret Munro began her private crusade. "In the beginning was the Word, and the Word was with God, and the Word was God. . . ."

"Matters haven't turned out the way we thought they would then! But all in all I would venture to say they could be worse." The speaker was Gran'pa Bruce MacAlister, and his listeners waited politely. Grouped round the kitchen table at the Mains farm, having their mid-morning tea and piece, a ritual that seldom varied from one day to the next, no matter what went on elsewhere, sat Gran'pa's "helpers." Dugald, in his usual place, knew there was more to follow.

Mistress MacDonald, who had elected to live in for the duration of the Cormack's holiday, rather than walk to Aribaig and back every day, still thought in the Gaelic, so she liked it best when the old man stopped speaking long enough to give her time to change his English into Gaelic for a better understanding. Her lad Roddy didn't care much about the talk, so long as the scones and tea kept coming. Roddy enjoyed his work, but he enjoyed teatime and dinnertime more. The minute old Mr. MacAlister gave the word, Roddy would be back at the job of whitewashing the walls of the steading.

They all were busy getting ready for the Cormacks' coming home, and some visitors were coming as well. It was beyond Roddy to try to remember all the different names and kin, so he did what his mother told him.

"Dinna fret yersel', son. We're all the same tae the Lord," she would tell him in Gaelic whenever he tried to name folks. Even the rest of Mr. MacAlister's story flowed above his head.

"Aye, Rabbie Burns says, 'The best laid schemes o' mice and men gang aft agley,' but it was said first in Ecclesiastes, 'All is vanity,' meanin' all our plannin' could be in vain. Some folk still say that verse means pride in appearance or belongin's, but I contend that it just means our plans are all in vain if the Lord isna' in them." Dugald sighed, hoping his friend was not going into sermonizing. He had been on his postman's route long before the usual hour today so that he could be at the Mains in time to welcome the expected arrivals, and he was having a job keeping awake as Bruce kept talking.

"According to the letters Dugald brought last week, Andrew and Elspeth'll surely be hame the day. Bruce and Hamish will be crossing the bridge oot there any minute now, driving their new house on wheels. His letter said he'd be on Tuesday's boat, and now it's Friday. They must've stopped in Mallaig longer than they thought at first. Eh, Dugald?"

Dugald jerked awake. "Aye, yer richt, Bruce, man."

Their meaning penetrated to Mistress MacDonald's daydream, and she rose abruptly from the table. "Mistress Cormack mauna catch me in the middle of a bakin', wi' the beds tae turn and a'thing."

"Dinna you fret, lass! As I was saying about plans, we dinna ken just when to expect them, an' they'll not care a docken leaf aboot the beds. Anyway, Bruce says he and Hamish will be sleepin' in their caravan and not in the hoose. As for Elspeth, she'll be that pleased wi' the spring cleanin' bein' so near finished. I'll have another scone an' some more tea mysel'. What about you, Roddy?" Roddy never refused food, so he helped himself as invited. Directing his conversation to Dugald now, Gran'pa continued.

"I'm glad Andrew had the plantin' done before he decided to go gallivantin'. Dugald, you an me'll take a walk up to the south pasture and see that the beasts are right enough. Roddy, go up and help your mother turn the beds before you go back to the whitewashing."

"Och, Mr. MacAlister, I don't need Roddy to help me wi' these beds. The feather mats are licht enough, an' I'll manage fine. Roddy, carry on wi' the whitewashin' an then—" Melancholy suddenly leaped up from her corner mat as the strange sound, for all the world like the kirk bell ringing, came to their ears, faintly at first but getting louder by the minute. The dog clamored at the door, and Gran'pa Bruce hurried to open it.

"It's Bruce. She disna' get that excited aboot anybody else. Come on, Dugald. The lad's hame!"

The minute the wheels were safely across the narrow trestles, Bruce threw the reins to Hamish and jumped off the caravan platform. A delirious Melancholy was first to greet him. Then, when he had extricated himself, Bruce and his namesake gazed at each other for a long moment before the younger gathered his senior up in an immense hug. Dugald waited for his turn, and he was rewarded with a hand-crushing shake. Soon everyone was talking at once.

"Any tea left?"

"Where's the bairn?"

"We thought you'd be here yesterday!"

"Where did Hamish go?"

Mary Jean, who had spent the past hour propped up between her daddy and Uncle Hamish, decided it was time she had some attention. Hamish lifted her down and handed her to Gran'pa Bruce. Tears sprang to his eyes at once as he gazed on the child.

"My Morag! That's who she looks like. Her hair's the same color, nearly black, and eyes like the sea. Nae color except what they reflect. If you had ever seen your granny, you would ken that, too, Bruce."

"Speaking of grannies, that's the reason we're later than I told you. We had visitors. All the way from—"

"Edinburgh. Aye, yes. Mistress Munro. She was here, and we directed her and her companion to the ferry. She would not stay when she found Elspeth no' here. With all the excitement hereabouts, I nearly forgot."

Mistress MacDonald emerged from the upstairs and joined the admirers round Mary. "Here, I'll take the chiel. She's needin' mair than admirin' looks the now."

Laughingly Gran'pa waved to her while introducing his grandson. "Do ye mind o' Mistress MacDonald here, Bruce? She and her lad Roddy have been helpin' Dugald an' me whilest Elspeth and Andrew are away. But come on. I want to hear all about Inverechny and what you're goin' to do now." The two disappeared into the parlor, with arms about each other. Melancholy, after one small whine at the closed door, subsided onto her mat again. Mistress MacDonald had Mary off somewhere in the direction of the bathroom, and Roddy clattered back to his pail and brushes.

Dugald was left to stare at Hamish Cormack. Not being endowed with the long-suffering forbearance of his friend Bruce, Dugald spoke his thoughts. "Ye're back then? A reformed character, I hear! You'll need to prove that to me, lad, and to the polis and some other folk in Aribaig. We'll believe it when we see it. The proof o' the puddin' is in the eatin', and in the good-book talk, 'By their fruit ye shall know them.' "

Hamish, whose discomfort had been growing steadily with every turn of the wheels bringing them closer to his old home, squirmed. Finally he risked a word or two: "Och, Dugald, man, ye'll just have to forgie me, as God says. I'm no' sure masel' o' what's happened. I'm sure of this, though: I'm a different man since I came through the watter. My life's no' my ain now!"

"We'll see! We'll see! I'm just warnin' ye. Dinna hurt thon auld man or yer faither and his guid wife, or ye'll have me to answer to."

"I'll away an' unhitch the horses."

Dugald watched closely. After a while he grudgingly admitted that, yes, Hamish did seem to have changed. His gentle way of handling the beasts certainly bespoke a reformed character. Dugald had never been given all the details of the shooting "accident," but he knew that somehow cruelty to animals had been part of it. Grumbling again, "Time will tell," he strode over to join Roddy at the whitewashing. The two Bruces would be a while. As for the cattle in the south pasture, their release up to the moors to roam for the rest of the summer could wait 'til another day.

17

"So you see, Gran'pa, even after Dr. Alexander explained to me how I could keep my thoughts private and still stay within the jurisdiction of the kirk, I just could not do it!" Gran'pa nodded. He had his own notions about Dr. Alexander and about the "kirk."

"It's called fence sitting!" He spoke so softly that Bruce hardly heard.

"Oh, I know 'Angry' meant well enough, and I did not deliberately set out to show him up when I told him that each one of us must answer for what we do ourselves, so although he'd not admit such a thing, I have this feeling that underneath he is secretly pleased with me. After all, he was my teacher."

"He has his place in the Plan, nae doot aboot that, but what's to happen now? As you ken, I'm no' one for peerin' into the future, but we've all got some concern aboot your well-bein' an' Mary's. Mind you, that contraption is a palace on wheels, right enough, and they horses, did you get them fae the circus as well?"

Bruce smiled. "No, just the caravan. Hamish heard about that from one of my parishioners or rather ex-parishioners. Some circus family lost the man in an accident, and the wife and bairn wanted no more of that kind of life." Bruce paused, and for a few moments the old man glimpsed something in his grandson's eyes he had never seen there before. They seemed to frost over, removing their owner from the present scene to a world unknown. It lasted only briefly, and then Bruce continued. "Since I lost Jean, I've not given much attention to money matters. But speaking of our situation at present, I must confess to a bit of curiosity on how Hamish is managing. The whole transaction of the caravan sounded too simple and too cheap. If I didn't know for certain that Hamish was changed, I'd. . . . Oh, well, I asked him once and received only a vague answer."

"Don't pry too deep, lad. The Lord has His way of providin' for His own. Rest assured it's the best way, and leave it at that. 'He doeth all things well'! I'm inclined to forget that mysel' whiles. Tell me more about the session and yon Alexander. I've had the feelin' sometimes that your 'Angry' could be a kindred spirit, but I suppose I must have been mistaken."

"Yes, very much mistaken, Gran'pa. He has one controlling interest, honing ministers for the 'kirk.' They must be the right shape and size, speaking in metaphor of course. Anyone not conforming to that blueprint does not pass his test."

"I still think you're ower hard on the man. That wasna' my impression at all. I've aften thought we could've enjoyed a good crack, him and me. If you hadna' told me aboot him goin' off in a tantrum after bein' the one to gie you the sack, I would have kept that opinion."

"Oh, well, don't be too disillusioned. I'm only giving my prejudiced side of it. We'll likely never have any further dealings with each other. The last I read in the *Gazette*, he was on his way to Canada on an extended lecture tour. He retired from actual teaching at the university the same year I was ordained."

"Ye canna fault him for any of that. Now what's this about you having your name in the papers again? It seems to me some folk get more publicity than others."

Gran'pa's eyes twinkled at Bruce, who responded with, "But you always told me not to believe everything I read in the papers!"

"Did you really say the things your mother tellt us?"

"Gran'pa, surely you're not suggesting Mam would make them up?"

"Not that. But she could have got the wrong impression. Did you call the kirk session a graveyard of whited sepulchers?"

"If Mam told you I said that, then I must have said it. I don't recall my exact words."

Gran'pa was peering at him under quizzical eyebrows. The older man was not sure if he should laugh or scold. "Nae wonder Dr. Alexander lost his rag wi' you and ye're mother's upset!"

"Gran'pa, is she still upset, do you think?"

"Ye'll need to ask her yersel', Bruce, and ye'll not have too long to wait! Listen to that dog. Open the door. I believe the other wanderers have returned!"

The wanderers had returned and in style. Aribaig's only hansom cab's ancient springs squealed in protest as it crossed the trestle bridge. Bags and cases were piled on the roof and spilling from the yawning boot. The reception committee, clustered on the doorstep, waited breathlessly as the cab driver placed a box for Elspeth to stand on. A gasp escaped the group as she emerged. Could this be Mistress Cormack?

"Mother?"

"What's wrong, Bruce? You knew I had legs and ankles, did you not?"

"Yes, but . . . ? Well! You look so different and younger. It's a nice outfit. I'm just so surprised."

Andrew, coming up behind his wife, chimed in, "And we didn't have to go to Paris, either. Your mother revealed her true nature when we arrived in London. Shops! Shops and fancy hotels and exhibitions and palaces. A body could spend a lifetime—and a fortune—discovering Paddington alone. Not to mention the Crystal Palace and some o' they other places you used to read to us about."

"Andrew, please, you're worse than me with your blethering. Save your descriptions for after. We have a bag of illustrations to show everybody."

"Och, aye, I forgot. It's to be back to 'auld claes and parrich', I see, and being bossed about. Oh, well."

The cabby was already being fortified with tea and scones, by Mistress MacDonald, who now had a request to put to Elspeth: "Mistress Cormack, I've done maist o' the jobs you tellt me, an' I'd fair like to go back wi' Jock here to ma ain hoose. Roddy can come again the morn tae finish the whitewashin'."

"Of course, Mistress MacDonald. I'll give you your pay and thank you!"

But Roddy wanted to stay to see the pictures. "I'll stay and finish the whitewashin', Mam!"

So the family, including Hamish Cormack, the returned prodigal, and extended to include Dugald and Roddy, sat round the table after the food and dishes were cleared away. Spread out before them lay the newspapers and pamphlets, produced by Andrew with a flourish from the Gladstone bag.

Devouring the pictures and exchanging remarks in the Gaelic, Roddy and Hamish were becoming acquainted. Andrew held Dugald and Gran'pa enthralled as he gave them graphic details of all the sights, sounds, and wonders experienced during the past few weeks.

"We even saw the Prince of Wales and his princess driving by one day!"

"Is that a fact now?" The listeners were gratifyingly impressed.

Elspeth had spent a besotted hour with her granddaughter, playing with the new toys and dolls. After that they set up Bruce's old crib, and Elspeth decided that Mary Jean must sleep in their bedroom.

This brought a protest from Mary Jean's father. "She'll wake you up early in the morning, Mam. You'll be sorry." Andrew glanced up then, but his wife was determined.

"We should be getting back into some good working habits then; we've a lot of time to make up for." The matter was settled.

Drawing her son away from the vicarious travelers surrounding the table, she led him toward the kist in the window nook.

"Tell me, son, about your granny and, oh, everything!"

"For one thing, Mam, she would approve of your new clothes. She's got some like that herself, although hers are a darker color and don't show so much ankle. Yours is frillier, too."

"My, my! You're observant, I must say. I thought you deep thinkers never noticed things like that?"

"Oh, I notice. Mam, I'm glad you're happy and not just resigned."

"Yes, son, Andrew is teaching me again not to dwell on the past. No regrets, but you know his sayings. When I look back, I see where he tried to teach me that long ago, but I was always too intent on—Och, well! Here I am doing it again. It's the now we have to think about. What else did my mother say? You mentioned she had a maid with her?"

"She did, not Aggie, although Granny kept calling her that. She's Rosie Ballantyne, I think. A smart girl, too."

"Did Mother tell you about your grandfather Munro, Bruce?"

"Yes, Mam, and he's bad. A living dead man, except Granny is sure he can comprehend all that is happening and is aware of what has already happened."

"I've gathered as much from her letters. But this latest attack—does she know if he'll live much longer?"

"Who can tell that, Mam?"

"She decided not to go off to London? What made her change her mind, I wonder?" Answering her own question she talked on. "Old habits die hard, and Mother always bowed to Father's wishes." But Bruce was shaking his head.

"No, Mam! That was not why she returned to Edinburgh. Not duty, but love!"

"Love!" Elspeth almost spat out the word, and the group at the table glanced over quickly. Lowering her voice slightly, she repeated, "Love! I suppose the same kind of martyr's brand of love that caused you to stand up and declare to your superiors that your ideas surpassed theirs. Men who have spent a lifetime in ministry and study, to be told that by a curate hardly out of school, a novice such as you. I still can't credit it." Words failed at that point, and the silence in the room vibrated with her angry tones. Roddy and Dugald had disappeared with Hamish and Mary Jean, to show Mary Jean the chickens.

Elspeth jumped to her feet, and Andrew walked toward her. Placing his hands on her shaking shoulders, he said, "We are tired, and it's been a long day, but maybe some things must be said, even now." Glancing over his wife's head, he nodded at Bruce to speak.

"I'm sorry, Mam, I knew you were disappointed, but I thought we had resolved all those matters before you left Inverechny?"

"I'm sorry, too, Bruce," Elspeth raised her head from Andrew's shoulder. Her eyes were dry and flashing a familiar fire. "I thought the same, but it seems I'm still harboring bitterness and resentments in my heart. Andrew here has asked me to be rid of it, and we prayed, and I thought I meant it at the time, that I would truly be done with it, but some things are not easy to do."

Gran'pa Bruce, who had been praying silently, spoke up as he joined the three by the window. "The way I see it, if we recognize our faults and admit we want to change them for good, we're halfway to winning the battle. Andrew and myself have different views on many things, even the interpretation of the Holy Word, in some places, but we are in solid agreement on important matters like caring about each other as folk, not as believers in this or that. Then God's Word proves itself to us ower and ower again."

Andrew nodded assent. "Right you are, Gran'pa. We'll say this then, and no more, about the subject. Bruce, your mother and I don't hold with you leavin' the kirk and goin' gallivantin' round the countryside in yon Gypsy caravan. Granted the contraption is very nice, but even if we don't approve of all you do, you are still our son. You will always have your home here,

you and Mary and Hamish. I . . . ," and to everyone's astonishment including his own, the staunch Andrew Cormack
broke down. Unsure what to do, they waited.

Soon the short spasm subsided and Andrew went on shakily,
"I thank the Lord for what He has done for Hamish. Many
hours of prayer and petitions have been answered withal! Eh,
Gran'pa? About you, Bruce, and wee Mary, too, of course.
When the time comes for you to want to settle down, just come
home. The Lord will provide." Elspeth sat quietly, her hand in
her husband's tight grasp. "Regardin' the kirk, your mother
is disappointed that you gave up so easy. She thinks you
should've pleaded for reinstatement and been willing to retract
a bit. We four all know a miracle when we see one, have we not
had many? But not everyone has that privilege. However, you
didn't retract your statement, and that's your choosin'. We
must honor it!" Emphasizing the last words, he glanced sternly
at his wife. She never ceased to wonder at how Andrew's
vocabulary improved when the need arose. He explained it by
saying the Lord placed the words in his mouth, and she knew
that must be true and another miracle, but being Elspeth, she
still wondered.

Andrew finished his words of gentle admonishment, "There
will be no more outbursts like that the now! I'll add this. Before
we settle down to the summer's work and the harvest, we have
one more journey to take. Edinburgh!"

"Oh, no Andrew, I couldn't. Could we not wait 'til next
year?"

"Next year could be too late, from what Gran'pa tells me your
own mother thinks. You will go. I feel in my spirit that a work
of forgiveness is going on in us all, even toward that embittered
and wasted old man who is still your father. It will be well!
Now, unless anybody has anything else to say that is edifying,
it's bed for us all."

But Gran'pa Bruce did have more words. "Let us pray!" The
four of them fell on their knees in front of the kist.

Bruce began with the verse from First John that everyone knew so well:

"Father, You say if we confess our sins, you are faithful and just to forgive us our sins and to cleanse us from all unrighteousness. We bow before You this night to claim that Word. We are fully agreed on it. . . ."

Their "Amen" was a fourfold chorus.

18

The word of the Lord came unto me: Out of the north an evil shall break forth upon all the inhabitants of the land. For, lo, I will call all the families of the kingdoms of the north, saith the Lord; and they shall come, and they shall set every one his throne at the entering of the gates of Jerusalem, and against all the walls thereof round about, and against all the cities of Judah. And I will utter my judgments against them touching all their wickedness, who have forsaken me, and have burned incense unto other gods, and worshipped the works of their own hands.

Thou therefore gird up thy loins, and arise, and speak unto them all that I command thee: be not dismayed at their faces, lest I confound thee before them. For, behold, I have made thee this day a defenced city, and an iron pillar, and brasen walls against the whole land, against the kings of Judah, against the princes thereof, against the priests thereof, and against the people of the land. And they shall fight against thee; but they shall not prevail against thee; for I am with thee, saith the Lord, to deliver thee.

Bruce paused after the lengthy reading from the first chapter of Jeremiah, and indeed the expressions on most of the faces before him could have dismayed him, if it were not for the last part of the quotation. Girding his waning courage, he began: "These words were written by the prophet Jeremiah, over 2,500 years ago, and describe Judah and Israel at that time. Their backslidden state! God promised Jeremiah that if he was brave and outspoken to tell the people, in order to have them repent and turn from their wicked ways, He—that is the Lord—would back him up and stand by him. I believe the very same thing goes for us today. This very hour as we are here together. The Lord has given some of us the same instructions as He gave Jeremiah. It is backslidden Scotland He is speaking to now. Here we sit, calling ourselves Christians, when all the time, underneath, we are rotten inside! That's what the Lord Jesus says about people like us in His words."

Bruce pointed in the direction of a spectator in the front row of the small crowd gathered round the platform on which he stood. They were just outside the gates of Aribaig's public show grounds, and the annual cattle show was scheduled to begin next day. Holiday-mood crowds, in search of a bit of excitement to replace their dull routine for a few hours, milled about.

"You!" The man glanced round. Intent on his message, Bruce failed to notice or hear the murmurings coming from the fringe of his audience. He continued to upbraid them. The man whom he had singled out watched him warily.

"Yes, you, how many times have you forgiven your brother for—"

The man spluttered. "How did *you* ken aboot my brother stealin' my best pigeon? What's it got to do wi' you? Who do you think you are to judge James onyway, a wizard?" At the word *wizard* the murmuring increased, and a moment later, an object flew through the air to burst in Bruce's face. Calmly he took his big hankie from his coat pocket and proceeded to wipe the remains of a rotten egg from his person. He started to say more, but it was useless. The egg was the first signal, and more followed quickly. Immediately the air surrounding them was filled with flying debris. Pieces of vegetable and fruit, leftovers from Saturday's market, joined the eggs as missiles.

"What's all this? What have we here? Move along now. Is it a free-for-all or a civilized meetin' ye're havin'?" The crowd quickly evaporated as the town bobby jumped onto the platform, beside Bruce.

Constable Neal MacLeod, Aribaig's bastion of the law, new to the town since Bruce had left for the university, took his job extremely seriously. As a rule his town was known to be law abiding, except that once in a while, on market Saturdays, he might have to work harder for his pay—on show week especially. But this was Sunday, and usually he did get some respite then, although with a wife and twelve children at home in the station house, you could hardly call it rest. Just the same, if he were pressed for the truth, Constable Neal would admit that the odd emergency call was not unwelcome for a change.

Speaking to Bruce, he shouted again, "What's the meanin' o' this, eh?" Before Bruce could reply he continued, "Can you not conduct your meetin' in a more civilized manner? I'll have to order you to move along."

"I am sorry, constable. I did think I could conduct a civilized meeting, but something went amiss with the crowd, as you can see. May we wait until after tonight's meeting to move the rig?"

Puzzled at the mixed twang, flavored with the usual peaty tones but overshadowed by a more refined accent, Neal asked, "Oh, are ye among they Shakers or some other religion that willna' lift a hand on the Sabbath, then?"

"Nothing like that, constable. We have no particular denomination, but we do have another meeting posted for tonight."

"Glutton for punishment, are ye? Tonight? I doot it, reverend. They'll riot on us if they keep up the way they did just now. What did you do to get the crowd riled up like that?"

The policeman now seemed to be on his side, so encouraged, Bruce told him. "I merely quoted from the Book of Jeremiah, explaining how the same advice applies to our day. One man resented it when I touched a sore spot, and he threw an egg. That started it, and you saw what happened."

"Sounds harmless enough to me, what ye said. Somebody's got it in for ye maybe! Anyway, I'd better keep my eye on matters when ye have yer meetin' the night."

Bruce, not too sure this was a good idea but realizing his opinion had not been sought, responded with, "I trust it won't happen again, constable, but just to be safe, I'll preach on the Psalms tonight instead of Jeremiah."

One phrase rang in his mind later as he ate the hot meat pie Hamish had procured for each of them. It was, *Just to be safe! Just to be safe!*

"Am I a hypocrite then, Hamish?" Hamish, his mouth stuffed full of the delicious pie, struggled to indicate he didn't think so. Bruce kept on condemning himself. "I read the Scripture from Jeremiah about the hostile faces, and then I turn about and allow them to terrify me. No! No! Even if I did tell the bobby I would not speak so plainly next time, I must obey my Lord's commands, no matter the consequences!"

Hamish looked out on the crowd as they gathered for the second time that day and almost wished he was his old self again. Then he would be able to protect Bruce with a few well-aimed blows and missiles. Not being a brilliant thinker, he failed to note that the old Hamish would be out there with the other troublemakers, ready to pelt rubbish himself, instead of being the preacher's assistant.

Inside, Bruce was on his knees, praying softly, "Search me and know me, O God. See if there be any wicked way in me. Cleanse me from all wrong. O God, I love Thy Law. Thy Law is love! I will keep Thy statutes. O Lord, forsake me not utterly. . . ."

Constable Neal MacLeod was a Glasgow man. Trained in a rough school, he also read every chance he could get, mostly the suspenseful mystery stories of one Edgar Allan Poe. From his vantage point, at the back of this latest crowd of listeners to the preacher, he began to use the skills picked up from both sources. For instance he could tell which hecklers, scattered through the motley throng, were not there from casual interest. He confirmed this when he detected a signal flashing between two characters he knew to be strangers to Aribaig. Wishing he had followed his earlier instincts to send to Mallaig for reinforcements, he firmed his grip on the truncheon and watched more closely. The man on the platform was fairly asking for it. Neal had not heard the earlier sermon, but if this was supposed to be milder, no wonder he stirred folk up. Realizing that he himself had been listening quite intently for a while, he brought his attention back to the crowd as the young preacher drove home his final exhortation.

"Behold! Today is the day of your salvation!" It was a declaration but not a thunderous shout. However, reaction came at once.

"Who do you think you are then, preacher? John the Baptist?"

"Naw! He thinks he's Jeremiah, the way he's always saying the Lord speaks to him directlike, but we ken he's only MacAlister fae the Mains, whose faither drank hissel' tae death!"

"His faither's the devil mair like. He tellt that man the day aboot his family feud, even though he'd not seen him afore."

"Devil's get, ye say? Let him have it!"

Constable MacLeod moved in quickly. Taking his stance beside Bruce on the platform, he turned to face the hostile throng. So he was directly in line when the first missile flew through the air to catch him squarely between the eyes. It was not an egg this time. Felled, the policeman lay as one dead. Bruce dropped to his knees beside the injured man. Quickly sizing up the situation, he called out to Hamish.

"Send somebody for the doctor, and then come and help me with the constable. He doesn't seem to be bleeding. I wonder—"

"Is he breathin'?" Hamish's experiences with the law in the past gave him a healthy respect for it, but he would rather be far away when one was attacked and left lying near death.

"Yes, but barely. O Lord, I wish they would hurry with the doctor."

"Could ye not pray, Bruce? Pray the way ye did in the watter thon day and. . . ."

Bruce hung his head as he answered, "Of course. Thank you, Hamish, for reminding me of something I should never forget. Dear Lord God, touch this man who, when he was attacked just now, thought he was merely doing his duty, but we know that in protecting us here in this place he put himself in danger. Without knowing it, Lord, he was being persecuted for You. Restore him, Jesus. We pray in that name. Amen."

"Well, well! I don't usually come running at a call from an urchin like this, but Neal warned me this afternoon there might be a bit o' trouble the night. Never thought he'd be the one to get it first, though. Where's the weapon?" Bruce picked up the rock from where it had rolled to the edge of the platform.

"It's this rock, Dr. MacFarlane. Is he bad?"

"Bad enough, but not terminal, I'm relieved to say. It will take more than a clout with a rock to kill this Glasgow keelie! Have you a drop water?" Hamish quickly brought a pan of water from inside the caravan, and the doctor proceeded to bathe the patient's head. His gentle touch belied his rough manner and speech. A moan from the injured man confirmed the fact that he was very much alive, and soon he sat up, blinking, slightly dazed but otherwise in command of his senses.

"Where'd the crowd go? I saw the culprit with the missile. I watched him aim, but I didna' have time to get all the evidence." As he tried to raise himself farther, the doctor stayed him.

"Wheest now, man. You're going after no criminals this night. Ye've had a blow from a rock much like yon that slayed Goliath, an' a wonder you can talk, let alone go chasin' a crowd that seems to have disappeared anyway." Aside, to Bruce and Hamish, awaiting instructions behind him, he whispered, "Could we get him inside your wagon, do you think? It's startin' to rain!"

An hour later the doctor had left, promising he would call on Mistress MacLeod and inform her that her husband would live to tell the tale. "Embellish a bit, too, no doubt." In his relief that it was no worse, the doctor took refuge in a myriad of words.

Hamish accompanied him as far as the livery stable. Dr. MacFarlane glared intently at Hamish once and then muttered half to himself, "Och, no, it could never be!" before he, too, disappeared into the mist.

Coming back with the horses, Hamish hitched them up. Then he walked round the back of the caravan to make sure all was shipshape. He almost tripped over what seemed to be a pile of rags. Quick as a wink, he grabbed the slight figure inside the rags.

"Oh, my, it's the pickpocket. Did you have a good nicht, then, or did the crowd melt away on ye?" The small body squirmed in the man's viselike grasp, and the hand pressed on the captive's windpipe kept him from answering. In fact he almost choked. Securing a tighter grip on the skinny arms, Hamish let go of the collar.

"I never stole nuthin', mister, honest!" The boy gulped.

"Oh, we'll soon see!" As he spoke Hamish turned the boy upside down, and holding him by the feet, he shook him thoroughly. A few small coins fell out but nothing more.

"If ye weren't to steal, whit were ye here for?"

"We were to shout aboot the preacher bein' a devil and then throw things, and Big Jake was tae throw a rock for the preacher, not the peeler. But I was listening to the preacher's talkin', an' I didna throw nuthin', honest, mister. I wanted to do what he was askin'." Hamish stood the lad to his feet, keeping a tight grip on the mop of unwashed hair. Peering closely at the small, dirty face, he concluded that the child—for he couldn't be more—was poorly fed and seldom if ever bathed. Suddenly Hamish recalled some of his own unsavory exploits in the years following his running away from the croft. He came to a decision.

"By, I think you're tellin' the truth, lad."

"Aye, yes I am. If I wasna', I'd be far away the now."

"Did ye mean it when ye said ye wanted to hear more of

Reverend MacAlister's words?" To their utter amazement, the young street urchin began to sob. Hamish, still such a newcomer himself to all this, was nonplussed. At last he spoke, roughly patting the matted hair. "Ye say ye wanted to do what the meenister said? Do ye still want to?"

"Aye, I do!"

"Ye can then. I'm no' a meenister, but I've been saved, baith by a miracle oot o' the watter and by the Lord for my salvation. If you're sure ye want to, chust say these words efter me."

Bruce stood in the opening, listening to the small drama, impervious to the rain or any other discomfort. Dr. MacFarlane had said Constable MacLeod should not be moved for at least an hour, and in the meantime they had both persuaded the zealous upholder of the law to lie quietly. After only a token protest, the bobby had made a mild joke of it to his doctor friend. "You're richt, Dr. MacFarlane. I do have a splittin' headache. Somebody should get after thon upstarts though, and I can direct the investigation from the constabulary."

"You'll do no such thing. Tomorrow I'll have another look at ye, and then I'll say when you can resume your duties. Now, if the reverend here will be so kind as to take you to the station house, I'll tell Mistress MacLeod what happened as I go by."

When the others had left, the constable had smiled rather sheepishly at Bruce. "I heard you praying, reverend," he said. "I seemed to be floatin' away at the time an' no' too sure I wanted to come back." He lay without speaking for a few minutes, then, "It's so nice an' quiet in here, and my house, wi' all the bairns shoutin' at once is—well—! You'll think I'm haverin', reverend?"

"Not at all. I think you need to rest, though. Just close your eyes. We'll deliver you to your house as the doctor ordered, but we'll wait a wee while yet." With unusual compliance, the constable had obeyed. That was when Bruce had gone in search of Hamish, his thoughts a strange mixture of prayer and self-recrimination.

Lord, I'm learning afresh every day how Your ways and our ways are so different, and I'm glad of it. But what could this be all about tonight? Certainly Constable MacLeod heard my prayer, but he thinks it all a dream or a laughing matter so . . . . He stopped as he heard the voices coming from behind the caravan. Hardly daring to breathe, in case one or the other heard and terminated this scene of glorious salvation, Bruce waited.

"What else, Mr. Cormack? I don't feel ony different."

"First you don't call me mister, I'm chust Hamish, and you'll feel different directly. My question is this: *What am I goin' to do wi' you?*"

Bruce recognized it was his move. "What's your name, son?"

"Jeremy Ward."

"Well, Jeremy, that name is just another way of saying Jeremiah, you know? Are you hungry?"

"Aye!"

"We're going to take the constable home, and then we'll be goin' home ourselves. Tell me, will anyone be looking for you the now? Your father or mother?"

The boy's laugh was filled with genuine astonishment. "I've nae faither, and my mither's in Glesca' wi' my uncle Frank. They wouldna care if I never came hame." The tragedy in the short sentence almost unmanned Bruce.

Hamish asked the next question as he returned from securing the rig for moving out. "How did you happen to be here in Aribaig?"

"I came wi' a gang for the turnip shawin'."

"But the turnips are no' near ready for shawing yet."

"I ken. We were to do some other jobs at the fairs and cattle shows." Wisely Bruce refrained from further inquiries into what those other jobs might be, and he signaled to Hamish to do the same.

"Oh, I see. Well, we have to leave the show grounds now. We'll take the constable home, then we'll stop at the fish-and-chip shop and buy some food. I'm very hungry myself. After that we'll be going to the Mains farm, where we bide sometimes. You can come with us. Maybe my mother will think of something."

"I'm strong, though I'm wee. I can do a lot o' things to help."

"What's your age then, Jeremy?"

"Twelve, I think."

"*Twelve*, is it? I would have guessed about eight."

From the depths of the caravan a feeble shout wafted, "Are we goin' to stay here all night, chitchatting, or am I to be got hame to my wife and bairns?"

Before Bruce could reply, the constable's face appeared in the top flap of the caravan's doorway. Bruce began to remind him of the doctor's orders, but the irate constable had gotten his eye on the boy still being held by Hamish.

"That's him! That's one o' thon gang o' thievin', murderin' cutthroats. You did weel to catch him, reverend."

Jeremy wrenched free, his instincts from birth urged him to run from the voice and person of the law. He did not get far. Suddenly he lurched and pitched forward, to land spread-eagle in front of Bruce. Neal was still shouting.

19

"Catch him quick. Slippery as an eel he is and fu' o' tricks!"

But Jeremy was far from tricks. Bruce squatted down beside the boy, feeling for a pulse on his neck the way Peter had taught him. The small frame began to jerk and twitch in a spasm.

The policeman continued to mutter about tricks until Hamish rounded on him, "Be quiet, man, the lad's in a real fit." For fully a minute the astonished Neal obeyed while Bruce loosed the ragged collar and pulled the boy's chin down. Then he resumed his shouting.

"A real fit, ye say? He tells fortunes as well, you know, and his gang are getting clear away an'—"

"Hush!" It was Bruce who admonished the talkative Neal this time. His voice held authority, and the other two were silenced. Bruce began to pray, "In the name of Jesus Christ I command you, spirit of lying and deceit. Come out of him now, and I speak peace to this child. Amen!" The jerking stopped at once. Jeremy opened his eyes, now clear and shining with an unspeakable joy. Astonishment kept Hamish and Neal from further comment as Bruce helped the lad to sit up.

"Can I hae somethin' to eat?" Bruce smiled in relief as Hamish went in to fetch a bannock.

"There's your villain, Constable MacLeod. A hungry laddie! Could anything be less harmful at this minute?"

"Oh, I'll grant you he seems innocent enough the now, but I still wouldna' trust him. I'll put him in the cell for the night, and the morn I'll question him aboot the rest o' his gang."

Pushing his hair up into a peak, to those who knew him a sure sign of his inner agitation and latent prayer for wisdom, Bruce asked, "Would that be wise, Constable MacLeod? Ye've had a serious whack on the head yourself, and your reinforcements might not arrive till morning. What about giving the lad over to my custody for a day or so, even just this one night? Then I promise—" Within Neal the strong desire to yield and go home to his bed—his head was fairly thumping again—wrestled the thought of his duty. What if this was a link with the elusive gang on the wanted list, which went round the fairs and shows, terrorizing folks? But he was weakening.

"Maybe you're right, reverend. If I have your word on it, then. But I'll be out to your farm first thing in the mornin'. It's MacAlister o' the Mains, is it no'?"

"Yes, it is, and you have my word on it. Now we'd better get you home to your own bed."

Elspeth received the news about the visitor quietly enough, sight unseen as yet, Hamish having taken him to the bothy for a cleanup. Jeremy didn't protest until his "valet" produced the sheep shears. He had not complained during the scrubbing. Strong lye soap had stung his eyes, and his skin, a stranger to any soap or even water, turned a fiery red under the rough ministrations. However, when he spied the shears, he leaped out of the tin tub, with an oath, grabbing them out of Hamish's hands. The sharpened points pricked his wrist, and blood spurted.

The ensuing rumpus brought Gran'pa and Andrew running into the bothy. The sight to greet them made them pause. A naked body, skeletal and ghoulish, brandishing a weapon and dripping blood, would cause the bravest to hesitate. The hesitation was momentary, and Andrew reached out quickly to grab the fleeing creature, receiving a bite on the finger as well as a bloody shirt front for his trouble. But he held on grimly.

"You wee fiend, I rebuke you in the name of Jesus!" As suddenly as it began the near hysteria died away. Gran'pa brought a blanket to cover Jeremy's shivering nakedness, and Andrew turned to his son for enlightenment. Andrew still marveled every time he saw the evidence of the Holy Spirit's work in this son who had been lost and now was found. Again he held his breath as Hamish admonished the small newcomer.

"You're in Jesus' gang now, Jeremy. So you don't say bad words like that. I know you got a fright, and Jesus knows it as well, so all you need to do is **say** you're sorry, and He'll forgie ye, but ye're not to do it again." The shivering morsel hung his head and waited. What would they do to him now? Should he tell them what one of his many "uncles," the men who lodged at their one-room shanty, had done to him with shears just like these? If they threw him out from this place, where would he go? Even if he could find his way to the show grounds, he didn't want to go back to the gang ever again. So Jeremy waited, wondering but no longer frantic.

The old man picked up the shears from the ground and placed them on a high shelf. "You can clip his hair another day, Hamish, but warn the laddie first. What he needs the now is some of that soup Elspeth has on the hob and an oatcake or two. She might even have some apple dumplin's left."

Jeremy's fears began to subside, and when the reverend arrived on the scene, carrying some of his own outgrown homespuns to replace the rags, the shivering finally stopped.

Hamish shrugged as he watched them leave. After all, what did a few lice matter in the long run—what Bruce called eternity. He walked over to the bothy fire and watched as the flames engulfed the remains of the street urchin's filthy rags. As soon as the fire stopped sparking he would join the others. Soup and oatcakes and dumplings. That's what he needed as well. They had decided not to stop at the fish-and-chip shop for two reasons: the constable might change his mind, and some of the crowd standing outside the hostelry looked only too familiar. Leaving the bothy, he sighed, and his sigh was content.

Wiser men than he could sort it all out. Some of them, his own kin, waited in the cozy kitchen.

True to his word, Constable MacLeod arrived at the farm bright and early the next morning, having ridden some of the way on his bicycle. He met Dugald, and the two walked the rest of the rugged path together. By the time they arrived on the doorstep, Dugald had heard all about the previous night's near riot, and the policeman had learned a good portion of the life of Reverend Bruce MacAlister.

Elspeth, having been told of the impending visit, had set an extra cup on the table. Bruce and his gran'pa pushed aside the maps they had been poring over and stood up to greet the visitors and introduce the constable.

"You'll take a cup of tea, constable?"

"I don't mind if I do, mistress. That's a long road, even on a bicycle."

Gran'pa showed interest: "Have you enticed Dugald to try that newfangled apparatus?" he asked, smiling at his friend.

"Not yet, but this is my first chance to talk to the postman since I got it. I'm new in Aribaig this last year, as you might know. But beggin' your pardon, mistress, I'm not here to make a social call. Where is my prisoner?"

"Prisoner?" Elspeth gasped, and Bruce came back into the kitchen, followed by Andrew and Hamish, leading between them the transformed Jeremy.

"Is this the 'prisoner' you're lookin' for, Constable MacLeod?"

"Yes, er. Ah! I suppose so, if this is Jeremy Ward?"

Jeremy had begun to shake and tremble. An ingrained hate for and fear of the uniform almost overwhelmed him. It represented the enemy and therefore was to be evaded always. He turned to run again, but Hamish, knowing a trick or two from his own dabblings in avoiding the law enforcers, was ready for him this time and quickly had the lad in a half nelson.

Andrew spoke for the first time: "Good morning, constable, I'm Andrew Cormack, and could I ask everyone present to be seated at my table while we reason this matter out together?"

He signaled to Elspeth as he said this, and she brought the teapot. For a few more seconds the policeman hesitated. Then with a faint shrug he resumed his seat.

"All right, then, I'll try to explain. You see, this Jeremy Ward is my only contact leading to this gang, and I must retain him in custody until I apprehend his accomplices." The big words poured out, and Bruce had to turn away to hide a smile. (Later Dugald asked the constable as they walked back up the road together if swallowing a police dictionary was part of the training.)

At the moment this was a very serious matter before them, and Andrew treated it as such. "I understand all that, Constable MacLeod. My request is that you allow Jeremy to remain here in our care until such times as. . . ."

The policeman shook his head emphatically. "That would be most irregular. He has to be questioned, and his testimony will be needed to bring the others of his gang to justice along with him!"

Elspeth intervened, "But he's just a wee lad. Will his testimony be valid?" Neal took a closer look at this woman, who, until now, had not been joining in the conversation except as she fulfilled her job of offering tea and food. What did she know of such matters? Apparently she knew a lot. Had MacLeod been aware that this woman was the daughter of Judge Hugh Munro of Morningside, he might not have been so puzzled. Scottish law had always been Munro's specialty, and his daughter, before her marriage and consequent break with her learned parent, had sat under his tutelage as he had poured much of his knowledge into her willing ears and eager mind.

Wheeling his bike along the road to Aribaig, in order that Dugald could keep step with him, the bewildered policeman was still shaking his head. "I still say it's most irregular. The miscreant will be off back to the gang at the first opportunity and—"

But Dugald would have no disparaging remarks about his friends. "Och, no, man, I tell you, when Maister and Mistress

Cormack gie their word, ye can depend on it just as you can depend on the sun risin' every mornin' at its right time."

"No doubt they mean well, Dugald, but I've dealt with thugs of every description. The ones that look the maist innocent are the worst. This one—"

"This one is far fae bein' a thug as ye call him. Och, aye, we all read the papers, ye ken, and see the illustrateds. We're no' as ignorant as ye make oot." Dugald was getting tired of the big words and the smug manner showing up in his new acquaintance.

"I didna' say ye were ignorant, Dugald, man, and I don't want to argue wi' ye. I'm just doin' my job."

"Leave this be, Neal! I've kent this family since the Reverend Bruce was a wee lad, and ye can rely on them doin' the needful wi' your, what did ye call him, miscreant? Besides he's been touched by the hand o' the Lord and is a reformed character, just like Hamish. You should've seen that miscreant afore the miracle." Dugald then proceeded to fill the gaps in the policeman's knowledge of the mighty works of God in the community in general and the lives of the family so recently met in particular. When they parted at the stile, Neal was laughing, and Dugald had promised to come out later and try the bicycle. Not on the common green, he insisted, but he knew of a quieter place where the ground was quite smooth, in case he should take a header.

Neal, with the vague feeling that somehow he had been sidetracked, agreed that they should meet the next morning at the same time and proceed to the Mains farm. Reaching the station house, he decided that maybe he would stop thinking of the lad, Jeremy, as a criminal. He'd give him the benefit of the doubt until he could prove otherwise. After all, he had lads of his own, and the thought crossing his mind by the time he arrived at the door of his home strangely reflected his seldom-acknowledged feelings: *There but for the grace of God go I or one of my own!* Meanwhile the inspector was on his way from Fort William, and maybe, with what Jeremy Ward had already told him, he would yet apprehend the gang at the cattle show this week.

Elspeth joined her son and Gran'pa Bruce at the table. The younger Bruce was speaking. "My call is more toward the 'isles of the sea,' Gran'pa, but it is goin' to be hard to go round them in a caravan. Only the big ports can take carts that size." Gran'pa was deep in thought, and Elspeth, having exhausted her arguments about Mary Jean going with them on their proposed excursions of evangelism, held her peace.

Finally the old man spoke. "There's nothing new about eatin' and sleepin' on a boat, you ken! Yon caravan is a hoose on wheels, is it no'? Well, I'm thinkin' if ye could build a hoose on wheels, ye can build one on a boat. Och I ken there's hoose-boats in the docks at Mallaig and other places, but they never move. I vote we build ye a boat keel wi' a caravan top an' a full set of sails."

"Of course. Hallelujah! That's what we'll do. If Noah could do it, we can. Och, Gran'pa, inspired, that's what you are."

"Inspired? Maybe. Mair like plain old common sense. It'll take a lot o' plannin', and we'll need the advice of experts."

"Experts, is it? When it comes to talk, we've plenty of experts about here. Ye're never thinking of taking the bairn on such a contraption as you just described? Bad enough to take her on that caravan, but on the water, what next? The caravan at least would be on solid ground."

"Now, Mother, we'll not go into that again. You know my feelings on the matter. Where I go, Mary Jean goes. You can take care of her for a while yet, until we see about transforming the caravan into a houseboat. This business about Jeremy will need to be cleared up, too, before we leave the croft."

Slightly mollified, Elspeth nodded. "All right, but can we reason a bit concerning Jeremy?"

"Jeremy is another sign of a manifestation of the miracle power of our God, Mam. In his own words the lad had 'the fits,' sometimes oftener than two or three times a day, if he got riled up, he tells Hamish. Since we prayed, and Jesus delivered him, there have been no fits!"

"But that was only yesterday. Is it not a bit too early to say he's been delivered?"

Both men looked at her, and Gran'pa's eyes glinted with a rare spark of anger. He spoke sharply. "In this house we have seen too many miracles to doubt this is one. It's a threefold one of body, mind, and spirit. It will take the mind—it being set on hiding and cheating to help the body survive—a while longer to prove itself, but our God is able. I believe it to be part of His plan for the lad Jeremy to be in our care—not just for these few days, either, but until he is ready for whatever it is the Lord wants him prepared for."

Gran'pa seldom spoke in this tone, but when he did, everyone listened and paid attention. Hearing the last part as he entered the kitchen in search of some tea, Andrew endorsed the remarks. "So be it!"

Hamish, following close behind his father, echoed with his recently learned response, "Amen!"

So Jeremy Ward found himself adopted, not merely by the humans in this family, but by the dog, too. Unable at first to comprehend the full significance of what seemed to be happening to him, he only knew he liked it. Melancholy licked his hand as he bent to hide his embarrassment when all the eyes in the room pivoted toward him.

Bruce saw the dog's acceptance of the stray, and he remarked somewhat ruefully, just as Mary Jean ran up to Jeremy, holding out a doll for him to see, "That fickle dog has Jeremy's measure. So much for a man's best friend! As for my daughter. . . . Oh, well! Father, do you know a good boat builder who could build a form of Noah's ark, using the caravan as the base?"

Not quite convinced, Elspeth sniffed as she called to Mary Jean. Then she recalled the family admonition to enjoy the now.

Smiling, she picked up her granddaughter.

20

But the law had yet to be satisfied, and Neal MacLeod was Aribaig's sole but staunch bastion of it, so the episode at the show was far from over. It had been one thing for him to leave the boy at the Mains but quite another to explain that to the inspector when he arrived next day in response to his report.

"We'll need to bring him in for questioning. As you point out in your report here, he is the only link with yon gang we're all after. The chief constable wants the ringleaders. There's more involved than just terrorizing folks at the fairs. They ply the local folk with the whiskey and encourage them to set up more and more illicit stills and distribution points. If we can catch them, Neal, man, we could both be in for a step up the ladder!" Steps up the ladder had no interest for Neal, but catching the gang appealed strongly, so within the hour, the two policemen were seated upon the ancient cab, proceeding toward the Mains.

Neal found himself echoing Dugald's words about the Cormack and MacAlister family: "I saw at once they were guid, decent, kirk-going folk, so I felt no compunction in leaving the young lad in their custody." A sound neither in agreement nor otherwise answered this, so he kept quiet for a while.

His superior finally spoke, "Take my advice, constable, and don't form judgments on the basis of kirk going. Have you seen any other suspicious characters anywhere abouts, the last few days?"

Neal examined his boots before replying, "No, sir! The town has quietened down since the show, and the other caravans are away to their next stop."

Inspector MacKinnon stroked his chin. "Aye, but they'll maybe be after the lad. He knows too much, I'd say. In fact I wouldn't be surprised if there's not a couple of them still herebouts."

Neal glanced round nervously as if expecting the drystone dikes to come alive with miscreants at any minute.

"Och, they'll not show their faces whilst we are on the job, constable." Neal began to understand why his companion was an inspector.

At the Mains farm all was in confusion. Elspeth tried to explain to the policemen, at the same time trying to quieten a screaming Mary Jean, while Melancholy barked her foolish head off at this fresh invasion of strangers. Thankfully the dog was tied up for once. It took a few minutes to get any sense out of the distraught woman, and that occurred only because Neal took charge of Mary by gently removing her from her frantic grandmother's grasp and simply giving her his whistle to blow. The inspector patted the dog before feeding her something from his own capacious pocket, and then, between whistles, they began to piece the story together.

"Gran'pa Bruce came round to tell me that he had seen Bruce and Andrew running across the lea field yonder, chasing after a strange man on a horse. Apparently the man had Jeremy up in front of him, although we didn't know that at the time. Gran'pa rushed over to the barn, and he's still there. I dread to think." A shudder shook Elspeth, but she rallied to continue, "He's taking awful long to come back, and I was just going to look for him when Mary started screeching. Then you arrived before I could think of what to do next. I—," but the two policemen had left her in mid-sentence and were racing toward the closed and barred double doors of the barn.

Inspector MacKinnon grasped Neal's arm as he reached up to

to remove the bar. "No' so rash there, constable. It could be dangerous. Climb onto that window ledge by the lean-to. I'll hiest you up." Neal scrambled along the sloping roof to reach the small, dusty window. Using his elbow, he cleared a space on the pane while clutching tightly to the narrow edging.

"There's a body on the threshing floor and another kneeling beside it. That's the auld man kneeling. I don't see onybody else, inspector. I think we can open the doors without risk." Still displaying caution, Inspector MacKinnon held his truncheon at the ready while Neal slowly opened the door. At once they were greeted by a shout from Bruce, Senior.

"By, lads, am I glad to see you. Yon scoundrels knocked Hamish here oot, and then when they turned on me, young Jeremy came from the ewe pen where he had been hiding and telt them he would go withoot a struggle if they didna' hurt onybody else. They busied theirsel's wi' him whilest I rushed oot to shout to my grandson. It happened so quick after that I can hardly remember what I did next. Och, aye, I ran to tell Elspeth, but then when I got back to Hamish here, I heard somebody barrin' the door behind me. They rascals could still be hereaboots."

The inspector had climbed the short ladder to the threshing floor. "Wheesht, man, we'll hear your version when we see if the ploughman has survived with his heed intact."

"Och, he's richt enough. I made sure o' that before I settled doon to wait. I gave a shout or two, but naebody—"

"The guid wife says her man and her son gave chase to the scoundrel, but you mention more than one. Did the wife not say she only saw the one, constable?"

"She did that, inspector." The policemen looked at each other and for the second time within the hour Neal glanced furtively behind him and around the beamed space. Nothing moved except the penned animals, and the inspector now had a different question for Bruce.

"Should the sheep not be on the moor this late in the year?"

"They should be, but we've had a bit bother wi' foot rot, and that's the reason we were all here at the steadin'. We've been dosin' them. Should we not be making tracks?"

"All in good time. I'm trying to establish if there could be one or more rascals as you called them hiding in here still, although I doubt they'd bar the door on one of their own."

A shout came from outside and immediately Bruce appeared in the open doorway. Everyone began to speak at once, and it was some time before a semblance of order returned, in spite of Inspector MacKinnon's attempts.

Quite soon, however, Elspeth's parlor overflowed with men, and Hamish was safely installed on the horsehair sofa, with the others gathered round him. Still very dazed, he was able to give only the briefest of details. Bruce told the story from the perspective of himself and Andrew, who had come on the scene after the fact, so to speak. Andrew put in a word or two here and there. Neal wrote busily in his notebook as the inspector dictated.

Finally MacKinnon gave his summary: "The suspects then, of unknown numbers or identity, appear to have arrived on the scene secretly at or about daybreak, possibly hiding in the barn until someone came to attend the livestock. Whoever it was seemed interested only in the young prisoner left in the custody of yourself, Reverend MacAlister." He stopped speaking to throw a glare at Bruce, who shrugged apologetically. The voice continued. "Disturbed by the victim, Mr. Hamish Cormack, one of the miscreants attacked him from behind, and the victim sustained a knock-out blow to the head." He went on to describe in detail the testimony of Bruce, Senior, and Elspeth, ending with the question: "No one has seen a second suspect then?" Heads were shaking all round.

He began the story from the absent Jeremy's point of view: "The aforementioned prisoner, after being victualized in the kitchen here proceeded along with Mr. Hamish Cormack, a son of the owner of this farm." He raised his eyebrows and this time his chilling glance struck Andrew, where he stood behind Elspeth's chair. Andrew nodded, and the voice continued.

"The two then entered the stable, I understand, intent on feeding the horses before beginning the day's job of dosing the sheep penned within aforesaid barn. I also understand that the horses were to be let out to graze on the lea field?" This time his eyes strafed Hamish, who moved to sit up, wincing as pain struck him. "No, no! Lie still, we can confirm your statement later. You and the boy prisoner, who I understand is unused to farm labor and frightened of animals, but nevertheless keen to learn, entered the door after you and slightly to your left hand. At that precise moment—Yes, Constable MacLeod, what is it?"

Neal was sweating visibly, and he wiped his brow as he said, "With all due respect, inspector, could you go slower? I canna' keep up."

"It's not necessary to write down every word, constable. You can fill in the less-important details at a later date. Now where were we? Ah, yes, at the door as Mr. Cormack walked forward to enter the horse stalls. But before you reached them, a commotion ensued, and you turned in time to see a stranger sweep the boy up in his arms and carry him off at a run. I take it this Jeremy was of slight build? The dog had commenced barking from the moment you shouted. That seems to be quite usual. You ran to the outside, but by then the intruder had the boy mounted in front of him on a strange horse—a hunter, you say—which leaped the low wall between the buildings and was last seen galloping across the same lea field, leading on to the moors." He stopped for breath, and Bruce spoke for the first time.

"If I may speak, inspector. The lea field does indeed end up on the moors, but there's a path leading to the top of the cliffs and then down to the sea loch. It's not that steep, but to town folks it might be difficult to manage, or so we thought."

"Yes, thank you, reverend, you have already stated that the horse and riders disappeared from your sight, but I have a couple of discrepancies here between the statement of Mr. Hamish Cormack and Mr. Bruce MacAlister, Senior. Sir, did you not say that the boy offered himself to the intruders if they promised not to hurt anyone else and—"

"Aye, and I say that we should be stoppin' the talk and gettin' a search organized if we're to find that poor, wee lad before something terrible happens to him."

"Your poor wee lad as you call him is a member of a gang becoming known for its many law-breaking activities, including such things as theft, causing bodily harm with intent to—and sometimes with success to—kill. More recently, they incited to riot. W , that is her majesty's upholders of the law, are determined to apprehend the whole gang. The boy is a mere pawn in this—" Gran'pa interrupted again. "He's a lot more than a pawn to our Savior, inspector, and we are bound by something more powerful than the law of the state, although we're bound to that as well. 'Tis God's own words. The law of 'love one another' comes first." For moments Rob MacKinnon had the grace to color, and he lowered his eyes. Memories of a mother saying those exact words caused a brief lapse.

"Right you are, MacAlister, however we still have to know all the facts and what we could be up against before we can organize such a search party as you suggested. It will in fact take the form of a manhunt, and the searchers must be sworn in as temporary constables and given weapons, along with instructions on when and how to use them." Hamish struggled again to sit up. Still half dazed, until now he had listened as one in a dream.

"Bruce. I think I ken the verra cave. I'll come wi' ye and—"

"That cannot be allowed, Mr. Cormack. You have already experienced the extent of the violence these villains will go to. No, we will take a search party of at least a dozen. Constable MacLeod, you will return to Aribaig in the hired conveyance. There you will recruit ten men and bring them here. With your permission, Mr. MacAlister, this will be our temporary head-quarters. Meanwhile I will investigate further and attempt to draw up a plan." An explosive sound came from Bruce, but catching Andrew's warning glance, he subsided. In a way this coldly calculating man had the rights of it.

His mother spoke now, "You'll all need food, and I've a pot of soup and some bannocks. Hamish should stay in here in the quiet for a wee while." Andrew smiled approvingly at his wife as the others moved obediently into her kitchen. Hamish leaned back on the cushions.

Bruce lingered for a moment to say, "We'll have to do it the policeman's way for the now."

"Aye! Ma heed is in a dwam, but first let me tell ye aboot thon cave—"

"Hamish, I know the cave you mean. We were there once when I was a boy, and you wouldn't let me go all the way down, but I followed you just the same. Anyway their horse couldn't get down there, and they disappeared in the other direction. The inspector would say a 'southeasterly' direction. The cave we mean is—" Elspeth's head appeared in the doorway.

"Bruce, I've brought some broth for Hamish. Should we not leave him to rest now?"

Bruce leaped up from the table.

"I can't sit here stuffing myself when Jeremy might be lying somewhere in need of our help. I should've taken the horse."

He rushed out the door, and Andrew called. "I'm comin' wi' ye. The meat is stickin' in my thrapple as well." Neal looked up from his second brimming bowl of the good broth. His mind had not been on duty but more on how he could get his Jessie to make soup like Mistress MacAlister's. Jessie was a grand wife and mother, but no cook. He pushed his plate away reluctantly as the inspector also rose from the table.

"My considered opinion is that it is foolishness to go out in search of criminals who, although to all appearances are kidnappers, are not. When you think on it, they have only rescued one of their own. We've seen the violence demonstrated on the victim yonder. In addition to go on the moor without sustenance is another foolishness. Thank you, mistress. Come, constable."

Bruce and Andrew had already disappeared into the stable. As he harnessed one of the Clydesdales, Bruce told Andrew of Hamish's idea.

Andrew looked thoughtful. "Aye, that's just possible. Even if they went the one way, we know of the place where they can get down to the shelf easy and go back toward the caves, hopin' that would mislead us. Now we can go direct to the cave ye speak o'. We'll take both these horses. Which is which, Bruce? Ye ken how I like to ca' them by name."

"Hamish named them. This one is Samson, and yours is Gideon!" Andrew laughed shortly but made no further comment as he mounted the bare, shiny back, but his hands gripped the reins so tightly his knucklebones shone through.

The inspector urged Neal on his way with further instructions for recruiting. Then he returned to the house and retired with Gran'pa Bruce to the cleared kitchen table, now spread with plans and maps. He shook his head at the departing horsemen.

"They're goin' against my advice, I'll have you know. I hope they don't meet with that desperate gang. I cannot be held responsible!"

The older man lost patience. "Nobody will hold you responsible, man. They're baith in the hands o' the Lord, and Bruce is God's anointed." Surprised into silence, Inspector MacKinnon turned his attention to the papers in front of them.

⸺⋆⁘{ 21 }⁘⋆⸺

"The boundaries of the Mains to the northwest go directly to the seashore then, Mr. MacAlister?"

"Not the seashore, inspector, it's a sea loch. Aye, I suppose the boundary line is the shore itsel', but it's never been stepped out or put to question."

MacKinnon raised quizzical eyebrows. "If I may compliment you, sir, you have a prosperous and thriving farm here, much different from many of your neighbors."

Discerning a scarcely hidden note of sarcasm, Gran'pa Bruce replied calmly, "We've the Lord to thank 'or that. He does take care of His own."

"Begging your pardon, but are your neighbors not under the same kind of protection as you, then, or is it a human lord, like the ClanRanald maybe, that you mean?"

Gran'pa Bruce did not take offense. "No' exactly. I cannot judge or account for others. All I know is that we, as a family here, do all to the best of our ability and according to the ways of God. As for the laird, yes, he, too, has been generous."

"Is there some secret code then as to how one should go about finding the 'ways of God,' as you so quaintly put it, or is it a case of 'I'll scratch your back, if you scratch mine,' the same as human collusion?"

Still smiling but becoming slightly strained, Bruce said, "No secret, inspector. Anyone can follow it. I have the rule book on the table here."

MacKinnon ignored that. "Did you not suffer at all then under the clearances and later on in the famines and harsh dealings from landlords?"

Sensing again some deeper reason for the questions, Bruce smiled sadly. "I'm my own landlord. The steading belongs to me and my grandson, but all the goods and beasts are Andrew's, along with his wife, of course."

"Still you must have felt it during the years when nothing would grow. I know someone—I mean I know of many a one—dead today or in America because of that."

"Och, we felt it all right. Being freehold, we only had to deal with day-to-day livin'. We had put feed to store, and we kept our stock free of disease. Then there was always the kelp market!"

"The kelp market? Oh, yes, between kelp and whiskey many stayed prosperous."

Bruce raised his eyes from the map on which he had been tracing out the cliff pathways leading to the caves. "Inspector MacKinnon, if you've somethirg to say, I'd be obliged if you'd say on. I canna' be doin' wi' thºse hints and darts."

"Begging your pardon again Mr. MacAlister. I'm overstepping my own boundaries as a public servant."

The older man waved his pencil stub. "We sold good kelp when the market was at its best, and we stored away the siller. Bein' teatotal, we neether support the distillin' of whiskey nor strong spirit, eether legal or other, in any form whateffer."

MacKinnon smiled faintly. "Teatotal, man? I'm glad to hear that. Have you ever heard of the 'Good Templars'?"

"I have indeed, and I heartily endorse their principles, if no' their methods of—" But the inspector couldn't wait. Enough to set his whole being aflame it was when his personal vendetta was addressed. Involved deeply in the struggle against what he, and thousands like him, considered to be the curse of humanity that came gurgling out of a bottle, he never missed a chance to expound on it.

Gran'pa let him rave for a few minutes before he noticed

Elspeth's startled face appearing round the lintel of the door as she and Mary Jean came back from their walk. She had heard the angry tones from outside. Gran'pa waved his hand in her direction.

"Wait now, inspector! I didna' say aught against the principles of your society, and I maun ask you to quiet down a bit. Mistress Cormack and the bairn are in the room."

MacKinnon's voice faded away, and he arose to bow stiffly in Elspeth's direction. She still wore a puzzled frown as she knelt to remove Mary Jean's coat and boots, but she said nothing.

"I beg your pardon, Mistress!"

"Say no more, inspector!" But her voice was muffled slightly. The strong tones of the policeman's arguments had brought old memories rushing back—memories first of John, Bruce's father, dead more than twenty years because of drink, and memories of Hugh Munro, her own father, a staunch supporter of the very society MacKinnon was exemplifying. Collecting her thoughts, she recalled her father, almost dead but living on in a prison of his own making, in her old home in Edinburgh. Placing Mary Jean's boots on the rack, she concentrated her energy on rubbing the mud spots off the soft leather. The boots had been one of her mother's gifts to Mary Jean. She bustled toward the stove while the child ran to Gran'pa Bruce.

"I'll mask some tea. Bruce and Andrew should be home any minute."

Andrew and Bruce tethered the Clydesdales by the simple method of tying each long lead rein to a rock. A few sparse blades of grass would keep the animals nibbling for a while. Following his stepson down the incline toward the loch shore, Andrew remarked. "Ye ken the way, Bruce, lad?"

"Yes, Andrew, many times we came here when we were lads. I mean, before Hamish left." Andrew said nothing as Bruce waited for him. "At times Hamish would let me go with him, but other times he wouldn't. On the particular occasion I'm thinking of now I had begged him to let me come, but he tried to chase me home. I followed him anyway, and I remember wondering what all the fuss was about. All I saw was a man standing at the mouth of the cave, with Hamish, talking away to him. I was worried about being so close to the water, as you and Mam had forbidden me to come here because of the tides. When the men disappeared, I sneaked up to the cave to see for myself. Inside was an old barrel and some twisted bits of pipes. I just ran home then. I understood later what it could be, but I forgot all about it."

They approached the cliff shelf. Now a steeper slope was in front of them, and Bruce slipped on some loose shale as it skidded out from under him. "It's eroded and crumbling here, maybe we should—"

"Seems safe enough, if we're canny. Dinna' go directly down. There's the path that way. It's a bit rough, but it's been used recently and no' that long since." They proceeded cautiously and in silence for another fifty yards or so. Then suddenly Bruce heard his name being called by a familiar voice. Jeremy?

"Reverend Bruce, I'm ower here!"

Moving quickly in the direction of the sound, the two men failed to notice the others until they were surrounded. A bunch of the roughest, toughest characters Bruce had seen anywhere since his curate days in the Glasgow slums, "the gang!" His heart sank as the ringleader stepped forward.

"Whit did ye have to come pokin' aboot for, reverend? We're goin' to have to kill ye noo an' yer faither here as weel!"

22

" . . . And although the highland clearances is a period in our history of which we're not proud, I believe some historians have painted it blacker than it needs to be. I'm not condoning it, mind you. I'm only saying it could be another occasion when God can take evil and make good out of it!" Gran'pa turned back from the window where he had been gazing out for the last half hour. His listener still sat at the table, and had Bruce known the man better, he would have recognized that he was speechless with controlled rage. His hands were clenched so hard into fists that he felt the blood wet on his palms from the piercing fingernails. His teeth ground together as he thought, *The old hypocrite! No wonder he hasn't felt any of it. He's been safely under the sponsorship of ClanRanald.* Honesty would normally make MacKinnon admit that the ClanRanald was one of the lairds responsible for much humane treatment of the victims of the famine and the clearances, but he was blinded by his own wrathful zeal. Innocently ignorant of all this, Bruce was asking for his opinion.

"Would you not agree, inspector?"

"Agree? On what? That your God turns evil into good for his favorites? No, MacAlister, I could not agree with you on that at all."

Bruce stared in amazement. "Och, I wasn't askin' you to agree to that, just on the fact that my grandson and Andrew, as well as Constable MacLeod, seem to have been away far too long. But wait, somebody's comin' now! I hear that dog. Before they get here though, concernin' your remark about good and evil, maybe we could have a bit blether on the subject at a later day!" MacKinnon rose from his chair so fast that it crashed to the floor behind him. Immediately Mary Jean started to cry again, and the dog's barking increased in frenzy at this further invasion by strangers.

"We can have no debate, Mr. MacAlister. As a civil servant I'm not allowed to have opinions on matters of religion or politics. Now I think the constable has returned with our search party, and duty calls!"

The search party proved to be a mixed bag. Neal had merely approached Dugald, who quickly rounded up men from the bowling green as well as some from the inn. Dr. MacFarlane had insisted he must come, too, and in all, nine men awaited outside in the steading when the inspector and Bruce stepped out.

They were quickly formed into three smaller groups. The inspector led one, Neal another, and the third had Bruce and Dugald at the helm. They were shown the rough map and the plan, and soon the three groups set off in different directions. Elspeth laughingly remarked on this to Hamish, when she brought him his tea, after repeating the doctor's orders to stay exactly where he was. Her laugh sounded hollow. "Like wee lads they are, playing at soldiers. Only nobody thinks it's a game."

Hamish moved his head, but the pain shot through him again, and he realized the doctor was right. He'd be no use out there if he was going to faint like a lassie every time he had a twinge of pain. Sheets of black lightning flashed in front of his eyes as he tried to focus on Elspeth, who was still speaking.

"I'm beginning to worry about Bruce and your father. It's not like them to stay away so long. Mary Jean, don't bother Uncle Hamish the now. He's got an awful sore head. As I was saying, Andrew would have made some attempt to keep me from worrying, if he could. I fear something must have happened to stop them from getting home. Oh, Bruce, where are you and Andrew?''

Bruce lay on the damp floor of the cave, his face down and pressed into the rough shale. A foul taste filling his mouth told him he was gagged with someone's filthy neckerchief. As he opened his eyes, they met blackness. He tried to move his hands, but they were tied behind his back.

However, he could hear voices raised in argument. One was saying, ''No killin'! No killin'! It's one thing to hold some rantin' preacher for ransom and another tae do him in. Thon fancy-dressed fella fae Skye never mentioned killin'. We were chust to get him away and warn him to stop his open-air meetin's and—''

''Wheesht, man, they'll hear ye, and there's mair to it than that! If we're no' to kill them, what then? The minute they're away, they'll be clipin' to yon polis. Dinna' forget the preacher's the one who came lookin' for trouble, so if we chust clout them and take them oot in the boat and drap them in the deep watter, who'll ken aboot it?''

A grim laugh from the other stopped him. ''Do ye no' mind how he can walk on the watter? His God'll not let him droon!''

''His God hasna' helped him this time. I dinna' see him gettin' oot o' they ropes or—''

''I'm no' an expert on that. I just ken I want nae part in ony killin'.'' The voices continued to argue, and Bruce decided to try moving again. Both his hands were clenched into tight fists, and he cautiously flexed his fingers to straighten them. At first the pain was considerable, mostly concentrated on the old wound in his right hand. Persevering as his captors still argued, he wriggled until he was rewarded by a slight easing of the rope at his wrists. Suddenly one hand came free, and he lay still to listen intently. What he heard was the gurgle of liquid being poured, and he guessed the argument must have been settled.

He worked his other hand free with little trouble and gingerly felt his mouth. The gag proved difficult to remove, but eventually he managed to slide it down and over his chin. So far, so good. A trial move of his feet assured him that without bringing them up to his hands he could not free them. Sounds of revelry reaching him from the outer cave were growing ever wilder, and he decided to risk rolling over onto his back. The sudden silence should have warned him, but when he opened his eyes to glance upward, he was shocked to see a giant of a man, dressed in a rough fisherman's jersey, standing over him, arms akimbo and a mocking smile on his lips. Bruce had no way of knowing if it was the one for or against killing.

"Ye're a smart chiel, reverend, but what are ye plannin' to do now?" Bruce's heart sank. The word *kill* had echoed and reechoed in his mind every moment since he'd first heard it. His tormentor still stood, leering, but Bruce was astonished to hear the words being hissed from the side of his mouth.

"Dinna' let on ye're loose. I'll untie yer feet. I'm not one for killin' onybody, but a meenister, naw! Get yersel' awa'."

Bruce gasped out, "Not without my father and the boy. And how will I get past your friends?"

The other laughed. "They're nae freens o' mine. Besides they're a' drunk. As for yer faither, he's ower there. Ye'll need to get him yersel', an' ye'll need to wait a wee while afore ye leave. Ye're on yer ain noo."

Bruce's brow furrowed in deep concentration. "Thank you, man. What's your name? The Lord'll bless you for this."

The laugh this time was less scornful. "Nae names! If the Lord is goin' to bless me, He kens ma name. I'll awa' noo. Mind what I said aboot lyin' still for a while yet."

Bruce had another question: "What of the lad? Where is he?"

"Ah'm sayin' nae mair, excep' he's no' here. The yins that came for him didna wait aboot." Bruce lay back to absorb all this. First the talk of killing, then the mention of a *toff* from Skye, then Jeremy. What was the boy's part in it? He refused to consider that Jeremy could be a party to some plot to kidnap himself. The turmoil in his mind eased a bit as he prayed

143

silently for wisdom and guidance. Soon the cave quietened down, and the faint sounds of drunken snores reached his ears. This could be a challenge, surely, but his heart told him what his mind would deny: They would get away.

He began to crawl toward the bundle that was Andrew. Loosing the ropes from his hands and feet before removing the filthy rag from between Andrew's teeth, he whispered directly into his ear, "We'll need to be very quiet. The gang seems to be sleeping, but we must take no chances." The other nodded, but a low moan escaped him when he tried to get up. Bruce leaned closer to hear his words.

"I think I've a sprained ankle! It's hard to thole, but gie me a hand up, and I'll manage."

"Put your arms round my neck 'til we get you standing up. Then we'll use the cave wall for support. Lean your weight on me. There, that's it." Laboriously they reached the spot where the sleepers lay sprawled about. Rough shelves cut out of the rock formed beds, and Bruce could smell the heather and bracken he knew would be layered across the spaces. Many times on visits round his parish in Skye he had found whole families, sometimes as many as twenty people together living in caves no bigger or better than this. But these men had not bothered to climb into the beds. His memories were cut short as a curse broke the quiet.

"Curse ye, man! Dae ye have to tramp a' ower me?" The escapees held their breath as the complainer subsided. A draft, faint but undoubtedly of fresh air, hit Bruce's nostrils. He had been holding Andrew tightly, and he felt the older man's breathing become more labored. Turning quickly he picked up Andrew bodily, as if he were Mary Jean. Moments later he stumbled out onto the shingled beach. A light drizzle was falling, but he ignored that as he heard a scuffle from behind them. Much later he learned how his benefactor had removed the ropes from the entrance and then replaced them after they were safely out. At the time he did not know but what the whole crew might be coming after them, so he made for the path as fast as he could with his burden. Glancing over the dimpling water, far below, he marveled again at God's diversity. The cave and beach he hurried across now were situated on a natural terrace formation well above high tide, making a place of refuge for men of evil intent as well as good.

Andrew whispered, "Let me down now, Bruce. I can walk by mysel' an' just lean on ye." Bruce half dragged, half pushed his stepfather up the steeply graded incline, sending down showers of shale with each step. His mind still dwelled on other occasions, when he had stood on the top terrace and gazed down in wonder at the shapes of the layered rock. A fresh groan from Andrew reminded him of their present predicament. From below echoed an angry shout.

Andrew gasped, "Go on, Bruce, lad. I can hide somewhere till—"

Bruce ignored this. "Up ye go, Father. We'll go together, and the horses will be waiting where we left them!"

—◦❧{ 23 }❧◦—

But the search party led by Neal MacLeod had found the horses.

Taking the middle route, as directed by the inspector, Neal and his group had left the stone dikes, where the plowed lands ended and the open moorland began, just before sundown. Instructions to mark rocks along the way had been followed to the letter. The Glasgow man had never ventured this far from civilization before, and his nervous glances around and behind caused some amused snickers from the others. Intent on the seriousness of the quest of finding Andrew and Bruce, though, they refrained from remarks. However, tales of the antics of the Glasgow bobby would be embellished and joked about in many a cottage and bothy for years to come. For the moment Archie MacBeth had to be content with sly nudges to his cronie, Davie Sims. When they did speak, it was in the Gaelic tongue, so Neal could not understand.

"It's glad I am that our lives are not depending on yon polisman. The lassies playing hide-and-go-seek are not so feart!"

Davie laughed uneasily. "He's no' that feart. He just doesn't know what to do or where to go."

A shout from the recruit flanking Neal brought them all to attention. "Yon's eether horses or a pair o' deer!"

"No deer in these parts, Willie, so it must be the horses." The

146

men quickened their pace and were soon able to make out the animals.

Neal spoke his first words in an hour. "That's the reverend's Clydesdales, right enough, but there's no sign of the men." Reaching the animals, he took another hasty glance round before saying, "We'll seat ourselves here for a bit of refreshment. Then we'll evaluate the situation." Not fully understanding the big words, but recognizing the actions, the others obeyed politely. When Neal opened his backpack to reveal scones and a sealed milk can full of cold, sweet tea, they nodded.

Munching on the buns and cheese, Archie mumbled, "Thon Cormack's don't hold wi' ale drinkin'."

His friend answered, "Aye, it's a pity! A wee drop wi' this cheese would wash it doon a treat withoot harmin' us a bit."

The couthy joke passed by Neal as he took out his big hanky to wipe his hands and face. He stood up. "Let us proceed on this path as far as we can go and survey—"

The spokesman interrupted, "Hold on there, constable. Did your inspector not say we should be reportin' at sundown?" Neal glanced at the sky as he recalled MacKinnon's exact words: *We will reunite at the west dike by this mark.* The inspector had splashed a large rock with a great daub of whitewash before continuing, *In the unlikely event that we find nothing, we will then consider whether to resume the search or wait at the farm until daybreak.* Sure that by then the missing men would indeed have been found, Neal's thoughts had not gone beyond that point.

He muttered now, "Aye, yes, you are right to a certain extent, but we have the evidence of the Clydesdales. Their riders must be close by."

His listeners were silent as they absorbed this, then Archie ventured again, "Aye, and Andrew Cormack would never leave them this long willingly. I would suggest we walk along the cliff top while the light is lasting, keeping in groups of two and within sight of each other. If we see no signs of life, we should follow instructions and go back to the marked rock."

Neal nodded, and they set off. Within a short time they were back, and Archie had more to say.

"What about the horses? Do we take them back to the farm, or do we leave them for the reverend and Andrew?" The animals had nibbled as far as their ropes would allow and were in some need of water.

Neal took a milk pan of water from his pack. Hardly enough to wet the muzzles of the big animals, but he bravely removed his helmet and filled it with the liquid. The horses lapped greedily, and Neal turned back to Archie, "What would you say about taking or leaving them?"

Archie asked the same question in Gaelic of the other two. A heated discussion ensued, then Archie said, "They say we should take them. They're valuable beasts and could be stolen, and what if Andrew and Bruce never come back?" Neal shuddered as the morbid fellow continued. "I say we should leave them 'til morning. So it's still up to you, constable."

Unconsciously imitating the inspector, Neal stroked his chin, trying to see the situation from the point of view of the reverend and Mr. Cormack. Suddenly his brow cleared. "We'll take them and leave a sign that it was us. Build a cairn, and I'll leave this other packet of food and the rest of this tea, and—"

"One thing's the matter with that plan, constable. What if the wrong person gets the message and the food?"

But Neal's confidence was returning, and he resumed his leadership. "We'll just have to risk that, and we better get started afore it gets any darker. In the mornin' we'll come back with the reinforcements."

"I just hope they're no' deed by then!" Archie spat in disgust and began to shout in Gaelic at the others. Quickly a pile of stones was gathered to mark the spot, and Neal tore a page from his notebook after having scribbled busily for a moment.

On the way back Archie ventured an olive branch. "Och, well, at least the daylight'll be up in an hour or so. If I ken they folk, they'll be sleeping 'til then. Just as long as they didn't kill them afore drinking, they'll leave them 'til mornin'." Neal groaned inwardly at this Job's comfort.

Flipping the curtain back into place for what must have been the twentieth time in less than an hour, a feeling of utter helplessness swamped Elspeth as her heart yearned far beyond her vision to soar out over moor and loch. The search party should have been back by now. That inspector had said sundown, and the last rays had disappeared quite ten minutes ago. She knew exactly because each time she drew back from peering through the windowpane her eyes went at once to the clock on the wall. Praying while she poked the dry peats into a fresh blaze, she swung the kettle into position. Another cup of tea? Not for Hamish, as she could hear him snoring from the other room.

"O God! Let nothing bad happen to my son or Andrew." Clattering hooves on the paving stones outside interrupted her prayer and she ran to the door. "Bruce! Andrew! Thank the Lord!" She searched the faces gleaming eerily above the lanterns. No sign of Bruce or Andrew rewarded her straining eyes.

Inspector MacKinnon's words confirmed her fears. "Let it not be said I did not warn your man and your son, mistress. Most unfortunate they didn't listen, but it can't be helped now. Meanwhile a bite and a sup for the searchers would be welcome. The search will resume in two hours, when the light is better. Constable, could we confer further inside? Thank you, men. As we agreed, you can doss down on the hay." Elspeth's questions died on her lips. The policeman's words and manner told her enough. Gran'pa Bruce detached himself from the others and, with Dugald beside him, stepped over the threshold, behind the constable.

"If you lie still, here behind this boulder, you'll be fine whilest I go and fetch one of the horses. We'll hoist you up on it, and soon we'll be on our way home and at the farm in time for Mam's porridge." Andrew managed a weak laugh, but he complied by leaning back on the boulder Bruce had indicated. The younger man removed his thick jersey and folded it under his stepfather's head before crawling out of the narrow, tunnel-shaped rock formation. Making his way carefully along the cliff edge, his own cheerful words came back to mock him, *Home for Mam's porridge! I'll hoist you up on one of the horses!* Getting the horse to come down such a risky slope would not be as easy as that.

Nearing the place where the terraced cliff hung over, his heart quaked as he felt the earth give under him. He stopped to get his bearings. Yes, there was the spot where he and Andrew had come down earlier. Measuring with his eye, he took a running leap and grasped the flimsy edge with both hands. To his own amazement he managed to hold on, and after his feet stopped their mad scrambling for a foothold, he began to work his way upward until his chin reached the shelf. Carefully he maneuvered his elbows into position, and with one more lunge he threw himself over the top. Lying there for a few seconds, to catch his breath, he managed a quick, gasping prayer of thanks before going on. The solitary rowan bush, noted earlier as a landmark, assured him further, and he began to lope toward the place where they had tethered the mounts.

The note read: "Rev. MacA. We have taken the horses for safety. Should you be reading this, you are still alive." Bruce managed a weak smile at this obvious irony as he read on, "Stay hidden and preserve your strength. We will come for you at early light. Leave a sign. Const. MacLeod."

So they would be rescued at dawn! Fine. He should make his way back and rejoin Andrew to wait for daybreak. As if on a signal the great golden orb appeared in the eastern sky.

But the official search party was not the only group seeking Bruce and Andrew at first light. Their trail was only too clear from both directions. Emptying his pockets, to provide the sign asked for by Neal, Bruce found one of the embroidered white hankies Jean's granny had given him. This object, a joke between Dugald and Gran'pa Bruce, at his expense, now proved a real blessing. One corner of the hankie was adorned with his initials, and using his penknife, he cut this off and secured it inside the note left by the constable, placing it back under the cairn. Then he tore some more strips, which he placed strategically under stones, giving the most direct route to where he had left Andrew. Hunger pangs caused him to search out a few edible roots, and he recalled noticing some dulse further along the path. As he slipped and slithered his way down, the sound of angry voices raised in familiar argument reached him. Was it all to be for naught? Had the adversaries, bent on murder, discovered his injured stepfather? Being careful not to dislodge more of the crumbly shale, he edged closer.

". . . An' I say we get away now. The farmer'll never mind us or ken us again. It's been ower dark for them to see. Let's leave it alane. It's no' worth it."

The other man was giving in, but he had one last argument. "What aboot the siller? We've still to get paid the other half."

"A dinna' care aboot that now. Nae siller's worth bein' up for transportation or worse. A think his God loosened him. He couldna' hae done it hissel'! A'm for hot-footin' it back to. . . ." Bruce strained to hear more, but suddenly the only sounds he could catch were those of half-a-dozen pairs of feet scrambling away down toward the water's edge. Within moments that faint but unmistakable scrape of a boat being dragged across the beach and then the splash of oars told him they were safe for the moment.

Bruce sighed with relief as he rose and stretched. No more need to hide or whisper. He called out, "Father, I'm coming down. A rescue party is on its way. They should be here soon!" An answering shout told him that Andrew was still in the tunnel, and at that instant a hail came from above their heads.

"Bruce!" Soon others joined Gran'pa and the inspector, who could now be seen clearly directing operations.

Less than an hour later, as the cart trundled them homeward,

Bruce told his story. "So although I'm glad to be alive and able to relate all this, I've failed to rescue the lad."

Inspector MacKinnon had a word to say to that. "A lad of that sort has a way of surviving. If he's what you say and is determined to change, he'll find his own way back to you!"

Gran'pa Bruce nodded sagely, but Bruce was not appeased. "I heard the talk, and the gang didn't go to all that bother just to let it rest there. More trouble awaits us, I'm afraid!"

Both prophecies proved correct. Jeremy would return, but he would bring with him some bitter news for Bruce.

24

Elspeth's porridge was a thing of the past, along with the oatcakes and ham and eggs and a gallon or two of tea. Her grumbling husband was now tucked up in bed with a bandaged ankle. Dr. MacFarlane had excused himself from joining the rescue party on the later expedition, so Inspector MacKinnon, after carefully examining the ankle, now swollen to twice its size, declared it to be only a bad sprain.

Appetites satisfied, the other rescuers left with Gran'pa's hearty thanks ringing in their ears. Seeing Mary Jean happily seated on her daddy's knee had made Neal MacLeod suddenly long for his own home and hearth, but his superior's words, as they made their way back to Aribaig, caused him to groan inwardly. No respite in view yet, it seemed.

"Now, constable. We've no need to listen to amateur methods of crime detection any longer. Mind you, they're a wise enough lot, I'll admit, but we'll proceed with our official reports and our next move. We gathered some valuable clues, did we not?" Neal tried his best to concentrate, but sensible thoughts eluded him. *What clues?*

"I'm more determined than ever to apprehend this gang, and you will help me, Constable MacLeod. The day is still young, and when we reach your constabulary, we will begin at once to put our findings together. There is much more to all this than appears on the surface." Neal's plans to stretch out on his bed for a few hours faded as MacKinnon continued, "After a while maybe your good wife could bring us some bread and cheese and. . . ." The rest of the sentence was lost on Neal as he visualized the afternoon ahead. Jessie would be thrawn enough with having to keep the three bairns, too young for the school, quiet while they worked at this conundrum, without having to provide food for them. His thoughts jumped to Reverend MacAlister. That good man certainly did not have his troubles to seek. No indeed, trouble seemed to find him, no matter where he went, and it flowed out in ripples to all who had any dealings with him. Pleased with this scholarly philosophy, Neal reached up to touch his forehead, where the goose-egg bump still dominated. Then he forced his thoughts back to his inspector's words.

". . . So when we have all the facts together, we'll be able to say whether this gang is working for someone higher up or if it's only chancing itself, with the reverend caught into it by accident. Whatever it is, we'll have the reason plain soon enough, and then it will be a simple matter to round them all up."

"Jeremy, it is. It's Jeremy, and he's with my lad Aloysius!" Inspector MacKinnon gaped at the two young lads running along the narrow street toward their cab.

"What now?"

"This fancy dressed man wi' the big hat on said if I tellt him a' aboot Reverend Bruce and Mr. Hamish making up miracles and such like. . . ." Stopping to glance at the constable, he waited for permission.

"Go on, go on, what else?"

"They wanted to ken how the big polisman, well, he said you should've been deed wi' yon clout wi' the rock. He said the de'il's ain, MacAlister, had witch's powers, and that's how he didna' get the rock in his ain face, and. . . ." A sob escaped the lad, and the inspector leaped up.

"This is a bunch of made-up rubbish. We're wasting time

listening. Constable we should—" But this time Neal would not be intimidated. "With all due respect, Inspector MacKinnon, sir, I believe the lad's telling the truth. You know I *did* get whacked wi' a rock." Glowering, the inspector signaled to Jeremy to continue.

Shaking visibly, the lad spoke up, "I tellt the man that a' the reverend did was pray, and he got awful excited, and then Big Jake, the boss o' oor gang, started to batter me. But the fancy man shouted to let me go. Then he said he would send me back to ma mither in Glesca, wi' a bag o' sovereigns, if I would just tell him more aboot the Mains." This time sobs shook him, and he could not go on. The inspector stroked his chin while Neal waited in silence. Recovering, Jeremy wiped his streaming eyes and nose on his sleeve. "I didna' want to go back to my mither's, so when they were still argyin', A ran awa'." His eyes implored Neal. "Can A no' go back to the Mains?"

The scene was taking place in the so-called constabulary—a long-handled name for a most humble room, barely eight feet square, with no windows and a barred grating dividing it roughly into two. Its one door led through to the MacLeod's kitchen. It was always a bone of contention between Neal and his wife, as he had always insisted it be kept scrupulously for nothing else but the jail. A hard bench with a pail under it represented its total furnishings on the side where Jeremy stood shivering as the interrogation took place. On the other side of the bars the policemen sat at the rickety desk and surveyed the "prisoner," each considering his story from a different point of view.

MacKinnon was in a quandary. What if the urchin spoke the truth and some high officials from the kirk were indeed witch-hunting for MacAlister? He could be in to something bigger than his first hopes of capturing the show gang. On the other hand, did he really want to know, and if so, what was to be done? The decision came down to whether or not to pursue this. In the meantime what should he do about this lad, Jeremy?

That he had been allowed to escape, or "run awa'," as he put it, could be significant.

"How many were there altogether, lad?" The slight change in tone caused Neal to glance his way while they waited for the boy's answer. Jeremy lifted up both hands, keeping the thumbs in the palms, without speaking.

"Eight. Three of them were strangers and not your gang, then?"

"Aye! The man wi' the hat was a stranger, too."

"They wanted you to spy on the Reverend MacAlister, then?"

Jeremy wore a puzzled frown, and Neal said, "They wanted you to go to the Mains and then clipe on the reverend to them?"

"Aye!"

"What was to happen then, son?" The inspector was weakening, and Neal watched the small drama with intense interest. His own son had quickly whispered to him that they had been on their way back to the house where the gang were, and he was sure it was close to the showgrounds. Neal felt positive he could find them. But they must do it MacKinnon's way.

Jeremy struggled with the right words to explain. "If I dinna' do what they want, they'll make me go to ma mither's. She'll be pleased aboot the purse o' sovereigns they showed me, so she'll want me to stay wi' her and the uncle." He had reached his limit, and sobs choked him once again.

Deep in the inspector's heart, memory stirred—memory of his own mother, on her deathbed, summoning strength to whisper, "Take the purse of sovereigns out of the china dog, son, and go quick before he comes back." She had stopped then, and the familiar look of terror had replaced the one of tenderness. When he had looked up, it had been into the leering face of a drunken stepfather, who had spoken. "A purse of sovereigns, she says. Wid this be the purse, then?" Dangling from its strings, the empty cloth bag had been a pathetic sight. Something had exploded in Rob MacKinnon's mind then, and he had jumped to his feet. Putting his head down, he had butted with all his meager strength into the bloated stomach. The man had collapsed in a heap, with the small virago on top of him, pounding, pounding, fists going like pistons. Surprise had felled the man rather than superior strength, and he had shaken off the slight form. Where the knife had come from Rob never knew or cared, but the man had suddenly become terribly quiet as he had slid almost gracefully to the floor, with blood burbling from his gaping mouth, astonishment forever etched in his eyes. The woman had lain half in and half out of the rough bed. She had no longer breathed. Rob had placed the covers over her, after pushing her head back on the pillow. He had kissed the still face, but he had had no more tears to shed. With the same cold logic that would stand him in good stead later, in his chosen but hard-won career, Rob had searched the pockets of his dead archenemy. He had been rewarded with two shiny gold sovereigns and a few smaller coins. Until this moment, he had never looked back.

"Yes, Jeremy, you can go to the Mains. I'll write a letter to the reverend, and between us we'll endeavor to keep you away from your mother and her away from you." Signaling to the constable to unlock the padlock, he reached for his notebook.

"When you ran away, no one came after you?" Bruce asked the question this time as Jeremy munched on oatcakes and jelly, while Mary pounded his back to hurry him up to come and play and a delirious dog yapped at his heels. Before he could reply, Neal, who had escorted him to the farm less than an hour ago, stepped in.

"Inspector MacKinnon reckons they wanted him to do just that. I know you don't like the word *pawn*, reverend, but that's exactly what the boy must be for a while—on both sides of the law. On your say-so we're trustin' he'll be loyal to yoursel' and stay on the side o' the right."

Bruce's brow furrowed. "I don't like the idea of him being in danger, Constable MacLeod, but do we have a choice in the matter?"

"We've had warnin' now, and we'll be watchin'. The inspector thinks it'll not come to that. He's away now to see the chief constable, and with the boy's direction on where to go, both here in Aribaig and in Glasgow, we'll rout the show gang. We've alerted the excisemen wi' full details aboot the caves and the smugglin'. We can leave that to them."

Bruce smiled grimly. Yes, he had seen the excisemen in action a few times. He spared a quick prayer for the smuggler who had untied the ropes. "What then, constable? Can we all live happily ever after?"

Neal shook his head in disapproval. "We don't believe in fairy stories, reverend. Within the law, we can only do so much. As far as the trouble in the kirk and its interest in you and yours, that's up to yersel's to sort."

Bruce's murmur, "God being our—and their—helper!" was barely audible.

Later the family did their own summing up, with Andrew ensconced in a chair, his bad foot up on a stool, while Hamish tried to be comfortable on the sofa, and Elspeth sat in her favorite position, with Mary Jean on her lap. Jeremy, the newest member, lay stretched out on the rug with Melancholy.

Gran'pa spoke to Bruce so that all could hear, "I've a feeling we've not heard the last from the inspector. He's a good man, but like many another, he's looking in the wrong direction with his hopes."

"You've a word of wisdom, then, Gran'pa?" The adults waited suspensefully for the elder to nod and speak.

"That I have. It's for all of us, and someday, for him, too. 'May the God of hope fill us with all joy and peace in our faith, that by the power of the Holy Spirit, your whole life and outlook may be radiant with hope.' "

Elspeth glanced up. "The Bible says that, Gran'pa?"

"Aye, it's in Romans. That's not exactly how the words go, but I'm sure that's what it means."

"I'll accept that." Andrew and Bruce said it together, and Elspeth smiled. Outnumbered!

She spoke now to Mary Jean, "Come on, my wee lamb. Teatime!"

25

"**W**ell, Charles, it certainly took us long enough, and the results are not as finally satisfying as we wished, but thank God, it's a beginning!"

George Bennett had hardly finished speaking before his companion gave a shout. "Thank God, you say? Thank God? I say better to thank Gordon and Carlyle, and a few decent members of the press for their heroic stand in this battle and—"

"Charles Booth, I would be most remiss if I didn't remind you of your own words regarding the Education Act. How did you put it again? Oh, yes. 'Life presents itself as full of chances, the best use of which demands free individuality.'"

Ready to resume his angry denials, Booth laughed instead. The friends were seated in the study of George Bennett's Glasgow home, their usual place for such debates. On one of his rare holidays from the business of reforming the social order, he and old George should be celebrating, not bickering. The Amendment Bill alone was a cause for rejoicing, raising as it did the age of consent for girls. This was more than a beginning. This was a giant step in the righting of the terrible wrongs within the social order. He and many others of the same mind had dedicated their lives to such causes.

"I'll give you touché on that one, George, old boy, but we both know I intended not to speak of your God when I said those words." George did not answer, and the two contem-

160

plated the flames in the shiny grate for a time. At last Charles broke the silence. "Your protégé, what's his name, MacAlister? Yes, he should be pleased, too, about the new law. Has he been up to any more escapades recently?"

"If by *escapades* you mean repeats of that unfortunate night you first made his acquaintance, I say no. That would be his one and only encounter with the demon drink. But if—"

"No, no! I meant the kind reported in the papers a few years ago. Miracles and walking on water and such. Then more recently I read how he cheeked up to the kirk and got kicked out for his pains."

"To answer you truthfully, Charles, I have not heard directly from him for a while. His wife died tragically, and that hit him hard. Mistress MacIntyre gives me his news from time to time, and the only escapade I've heard of since the one you mentioned concerns an occasion when he tackled some smugglers almost single-handed, and he helped the police to round up a gang of cutthroat hecklers. Of course his friend Dr. Blair gave me that news, and he could be embellishing a bit."

"You know, George, along with yourself and Miss Amelia Godfrey, that young man could be one of the few who might help to restore mankind to a semblance of what I learned in my youth to consider divine."

George placed his coffee cup carefully on the tray before answering. Could he be hearing right? "Why, Charles, I'm delighted to hear you say that. I am indeed!"

"You mean you never thought you would hear me say anything positive pertaining to religion, don't you, George? To tell you the truth I've been doing a bit of thinking between debates and in the times of waiting for votes to be counted, and I find myself agreeing with some of your theories. Not all by any means, mind you, but some. For instance, perhaps the failure of Christianity is indeed the fault of the churches and not the one for whom it is named! What a pity there are not more MacAlisters or Bennetts or Godfreys about."

"There could be at least one more, Charles!"

"As I said, George, I have been thinking, but even with what I've just mentioned, I don't, well, I would need to think a lot more. The whole business sounds too easy the way you and the MacAlister chieftain describe it. The existence of a personal God still seems a bit too farfetched to me. A Supreme Being I'll admit to, but a Being interested in our small doings, hardly. Think of a decent human being allowing someone, say like that so-called mother in the court the other day, to barter her tiny girls for men's amusement and her own gain. No, George, there are still too many unanswered questions."

"I know, but Charles, can you not see that's just the thing. Changes have to take place within individuals, and that only happens after the individuals themselves give God permission to work in their lives. He will not force us. Oh, Charles, my good friend, I implore you to think again. Think deeply on it. The Lord needs men such as you! Strong men with a vision. Even your thinking means that deep within yourself you are seeking God, and He will not disappoint you."

Charles had moved to the sideboard during this speech, but now he turned back without touching the brandy bottle. "All very mystical, I'm sure, George, and I know you are sincere, but believe me, if I had this calling, or whatever it is you are talking about, I would know. When or if that happens, you will be the first to hear about it. No, at present I am quite content to take each day as it comes, helping those less fortunate when I have the opportunity. You are always saying I should keep my mind open, and I'll try, but I agree with your Scottish bard who puts it very well: 'That man to man the world o'er, shall brithers be, for a' that'!" Laughing, he walked back to the sideboard, and this time he filled a glass and drained it.

George did not join the laughter. Instead his lips moved in silent prayer. "Oh Jerusalem, Jerusalem. How oft would I have gathered thy children together, and you would not?"

The fire died down, and still they sat on. Finally George rose.

"Good night, Charles, I'm glad you can stay for a day or two longer this time."

"Good night, George. Don't blame yourself for my sorry state. Perhaps I like the way I am and have no desire to change? The unreformed reformer, eh?"

Serving breakfast, next morning, a surprised Mistress Oliver reported back to the cook. "My, it's like a funeral in there this mornin'. Nae jokes nor even talkin'. I wonder if they've fell oot?"

"The gentry don't fa' oot. It's mair likely that Mr. Booth's emptied the maister's whiskey bottle and has a heid on him. I'm aye that surprised when Mr. Bennett orders the whiskey and such when he's expectin' Mr. Booth. You'd think. . . . Aye, weel, it's no' our business."

Mistress Oliver agreed to that and would have left it there, but the cook had further enlightenment.

"The whiskey gives ye the fun and the jokes the first time, but when it comes back on ye next day, it's no' sae funny. I mind the time when my Tam. . . ."

Cook's rememberings went unheeded as Mistress Oliver continued to wonder out loud. "Their talk was about young Reverend MacAlister last night. You weren't here, so you'll not recall when he stayed wi' us that time. Mr. Booth and him never got on. It was one of they clashes o' personality, hate at first sight you might say and yet. . . . Och, well, we canna make a better of it, so I'll just take in the coffee; then we can have our own breakfast peacefu'like without the bell ringin'."

Not to be done out of her story-telling, the cook began again as soon as the two were seated to their own abundant meal. "Mark my words, Sally, it's conveection, that's what it is. I ken fine, for I saw my Tam afore he would gie in tae the Lord, and that on his deathbed, the stubborn auld fool. Och, aye. Lord forgie me, and I thank You for savin' him before the end!"

George Bennett's mind seethed with self-blame as he helped himself to a cup of the steaming fresh brew, after first pouring one for Charles. In spite of his admonishing himself not to take on condemnation, he still did.

His discomfort was only too apparent to his guest, but Charles solved the situation. "Great breakfast drink, this coffee, I learned how to drink it without milk or sugar when I was in America—the States they like to be called now—but I must confess I like it better with a spot of fresh cream, like this." He poured the cream liberally as he spoke.

George acknowledged the compliment with a negligent wave of his hand. "Don't mention it. Just enjoy it. Last night you spoke of Bruce MacAlister, and not strangely, I dreamed of him after that. Now, however, comes the strange part. Mistress MacIntyre sent me a note this morning. It appears her I suppose you could say grandson-in-law, although it's quite a mouthful, along with his retinue will be arriving in Glasgow this very week. He asked her to inform me of this and also to tell me that he would be willing to speak at our meeting this Sunday."

Charles glanced quizzically at his friend, over the top of his spectacles. The statement did not require a reply, but he furnished one anyway. "Is that a fact? You know, George, old chap, I must admit I am curious. Although the highland chieftain and I did not hit it off, I still think there's something, well, I have to say, *special* about him. A regal bearing not common even among so-called royalty. Would you, I mean could we, arrange something? I would like to hear him just once. Incognito, mind you, otherwise, no! You do understand it's only out of curiosity, of course?"

"Of course, of course, I promise. Man, you can sit away at the back, and I'll make no mention whatever, and. . . ." Completely overcome, George turned away for a moment. His delight was pouring down his cheeks in the form of real tears at this unexpected eventuality. Then, after absently patting Charles on the shoulder, he rushed to the door, calling back, "Must get a note to Beulah and one to our deacon board, about Bruce, at once."

26

"She hasna' Miss Jean's red hair at all, and her wee pug nose, where did that come from, I wonder?" Cook Mac-Laren and Betsy were inventorying Mary Jean as they did each year when the group arrived from the north.

"Och, Cook, she's just hersel'. Wi' eyes like that she can rule the roost anywhere and especially this roost here."

"All the same, Betsy, she does hae that froon. Ye mind when he would sit wi' the books, twistin' his hair roon' his finger and froonin' like yer washin' board?"

Betsy remembered.

Strathcona House rang with preparations for another celebration. This occasion was Mary Jean MacAlister's fifth birthday.

In the parlor Beulah almost echoed Betsy's words before saying, "Why is it she has none of your coloring, yet she resembles you so closely?" Bruce laughed at Jean's granny.

"I don't know, Great-grandmother MacIntyre, but I see what you mean right enough. That dark-brown hair—mind you, it does have reddish glints in certain lights—those dark-gray eyes, the pug nose, and fair skin. Genetics never was a subject I cared to study much, and I know the Lord has every hair counted. I wonder what Dr. Peter would have to say if we asked him?"

"We'll not be asking him. Remember that time we mentioned the subject at table and he gave us a lecture as long as your arm, and nobody ate their rice pudding with raisins." They chuckled together.

"I still can hardly believe Peter is a married man himself, now, and a father, too, with twin sons already. Granny Mac, I've been meaning to ask you, since Peter and Agatha's wedding. I know she's Faye Felicity's niece, but had I ever met her before? Before we came for the wedding, I mean. She seemed so familiar, yet it keeps eluding me, like a dream you cannot quite recall."

Beulah's eyes clouded and she turned away to gaze out the window for a moment before venturing to reply, "Yes, Bruce, you met her. She came with us to Skye for Jean's, that time we—ah—but even before that she attended the reception here and—" Beulah could not continue, and neither spoke for a short time.

Bruce crossed over to the old lady's chair. Placing his hands on her shoulders he said, "Now I remember. I wasn't very polite to her, or any of you for that matter, was I, Granny Mac? But it is all right to grieve for loved ones. God revealed much to me while I was in the pit of my sorrow. One thing stays clear. Our Jean is with Him, helping Him in ways we are not allowed to know yet. We're not to sit idly and wait to go to her and to Him, should He not return soon, nor is she sitting playing on a harp all the time. I recall vaguely a knowing coming into my spirit that she is doing greater works, which we cannot yet comprehend." The silence deepened in the room. These two, closest to the one they spoke of now, had never been together in this way before.

Mary Jean sat in a corner, playing with her many dolls. A new one from Auntie Faye in India had been waiting for her here, as well as one, dressed in the Munro tartan from her other great-granny. The child sat on while her daddy and Granny Mac talked. She heard the name *Jean* many times, and she knew that was her mammy's name. Then they talked about Uncle Peter and the twins. Mary Jean knew these were not real cousins, and she was glad about that, because the twins could be meanies sometimes. When Betsy came in to announce that Dr. Peter and his family had arrived, Mary Jean sighed. This had been nice, and now the party would begin, and even if it was her own birthday, she liked it better when she and Daddy and Granny Mac sat at the table together. Now she would have to sit in the kitchen with the twins and their nanny and Betsy, and oh, well, her Uncle Hamish would be there, too. He knew.

Although wrong about having to sit in the kitchen, Mary Jean was correct about the noise. Uncle Peter started it by roaring, but she liked him anyway.

"There you are, my hieland laddie! Still at it, I see. When are you going to come back and live in a civilized manner again?"

Peter continued to work at the clinic, but he now had a private practice as well. He never missed an opportunity to try to convince Bruce he should be working in Glasgow.

Peter's conversion had been settled finally to everyone's satisfaction when Agatha Rose's wealthy Yorkshire parents, tired of her relentless moping and indecisions, came to Glasgow with their ultimatum. The couple had one private matter to settle before Agatha would allow the wedding date to be set: her fear of having babies. This soon evaporated when Peter stipulated some conditions of his own concerning their marriage and told her some facts about childbirth, showing her pictures from his medical textbooks. After he promised he would not leave her side for the last few weeks, when her time came, she gave in and at last agreed to marry him.

Shortly after that, the wedding, a complete contrast to Jean and Bruce's, took place.

An ideal situation declared Dr. Blair, Senior. They loved each other in a businesslike fashion—give a little, take a little. If he had reservations about his son's conversion, he kept them to himself.

Who knew better than he, and from personal experience, that instant changes were entirely possible. His own emancipation from drink had happened immediately following an autopsy he had to perform on a patient whose death at first seemed mysterious. The man had been found hanging from a rafter, strung up in his own necktie. At the postmortem Dr. Blair saw for the first time a close-up of an alcohol-rotted liver, and he had not touched the whiskey or any other alcoholic beverage since that day.

He moved about restlessly now as he considered his reason for being in Glasgow at this time—a medical convention he, and he hoped his son, too, would attend tomorrow in the Grass Market, which concerned the diseases related to drink. His visit coincided with the MacAlister bairn's birthday, so he had been included in the invitation, with his son's family.

The groups seated about in Beulah's parlor had merely gravitated toward one another. George and Beulah, close to the fireplace, discussed Charles Booth and the latest surprise coming from that source. George had sworn Beulah to secrecy about the plan to smuggle Charles into the meeting tomorrow. So they sat like the pair of conspirators they undoubtedly were.

On the other side of the fireplace huddled Agatha Rose Blair. Although her husband was on the rug at her feet, rubbing away at her pain-filled ankles, she knew she might as well be alone for all he or Bruce MacAlister noticed. She was tired and poor company indeed, being so far along. She listened to the talk, though, as Bruce described his habitation—the houseboat, or *Revelation* as he called it, plying between the isles away up there, close to that desolate place she remembered with such horror. You would have thought Bruce MacAlister had had enough of the ocean and those dreadful islands. Agatha shivered, forcing her thoughts away from the Isle of Skye and all it reminded her of. As always she cried too easily, and she was enough of a frightful sight at the moment. Her attention came back to the men as Bruce was telling Peter most enthusiastically about the boat's sails.

"Peter, old son, you knew we named the boat *Revelation* the day she was launched. But we really got inspired—or I should say Hamish got inspired—when he read from Isaiah one day, the very Scripture verse that gave me my idea in the first place.

Isaiah twenty-four it is, and verse fifteen: 'Wherefore glorify ye the Lord in the fires, even the name of the Lord God of Israel in the isles of the sea.' "

"It still beats me how you can reach your conclusions about what God is saying to you and how you can turn round and compose a sermon that would make the statues out there in the park want to be saved."

"Not me, man, that's the Holy Spirit. He only uses me 'cause I'm willing to be used."

"See what I mean? Coming from anybody else, that would sound sanctimonious, but from you I know it's real."

"Well, the boat sails have that verse I just said written up on them, for all the isles to view."

"Every word?"

"Every word. Hamish paints them on, and when he finishes one end, he just starts again at the other."

Dr. Blair, Senior, followed the children back to the kitchen. Never had there been such wonders as these twins, as millions of grandfathers before him and millions after him no doubt thought of their own. What braw lads they were, though. He wasn't one for bragging, but Mary Jean MacAlister was a wee plain Jane beside them. Glancing from one to the other, the besotted grandfather complacently smiled to himself. Just then Mary Jean turned toward him, giving him the full benefit of her glorious eyes. *Not so plain after all*, he decided. *Most assuredly not plain. What eyes!* The martinet of a nurse swooped down on the children at that moment, and the grandfather relinquished them. Faces had to be washed and so on, as the carriage was coming in five minutes.

The leave taking was over, and someone had taken Mary Jean off to her bed, complete with loaded basket of dolls and other new toys. Dr. Blair found himself with nothing to do but wait in the kitchen for the carriage to come back for him. Soon the servants were eyeing him, expecting him to leave. After a long, hard day, they didn't need any gentry invading their domain. Ignoring this obvious resentment, he walked toward the table and sat down.

Cook MacLaren, taking advantage of her privileged position, dared a question. "Was there no room for you in the carriage, doctor?"

"No, my daughter-in-law takes up enough room for three or more, and with the nurse and all the paraphernalia . . . !" Cook sniffed. It was all right for her and Betsy to criticize the nurse, but coming from the gentry it was different. The intruder continued. "I will await my son. The carriage had to make two journeys to bring us, you may recall."

Hamish reclaimed his own seat at the kitchen table, after having assured himself that Mary Jean was settled for the night. The old doctor talked on: "You're the fellow who walked on the water, are you not?"

Betsy gasped, *The cheeky thing!*

Hamish didn't seem to care. "Aye, some say that, but we didna' walk on the water."

"The story was a hoax then?"

"Not at all! We spent the whole nicht in the watter, and Bruce felt the strength o' the Lord sustainin' him and keepin' him able to 'tread watter.' I dinna swim masel', so I'm no' sure whit that means."

"It means not walking on water exactly, but that's a close enough way of puttin' it; and if the water was ice cold, as I've heard tell, you should both be dead. No one treads water all night without—"

"As I said, the help o' the Holy Spirit." Hamish subsided as though the conversation were finished. As far as he was concerned it was. But the doctor had more to say.

"I've aye thought, since I heard yon story and knowing Bruce wouldna' tell a lie, that I wanted to hear the right of it. Peter would never say."

"Well, for mair than I've tellt ye, ye'll need to ask Bruce."

"Are you truly his brother, then, as one report said?"

"My, my, doctor! Ye're the one for the questions. My father,

Andrew Cormack, is wed to his mother, Elspeth. I dinna ken if that maks us brithers, but we've a closer tie." Silence reigned in the warm kitchen as the other occupants absorbed all this. They had heard the story but never before from Hamish.

Suddenly Dr. Blair leapt to his feet, upsetting the chair as he went. His words as he rushed out sounded like, "I must look into this further, maybe Bruce MacAlister's God, and now my Peter's God, too, is real."

The three round the table gaped at each other, and as he righted the chair Hamish said, "Hallelujah! That's their first step, and now he'll ask Bruce or somebody else who kens, and he'll find the Lord for hissel'." Not hallelujah shouters, the other two nevertheless nodded wisely.

"It's about time, too! Now, Hamish, we want to hear more aboot that ship. What do you mean, you paint words on the sails? It sounds awful silly to me!"

"It's no' silly, lassie. The words are fae the Holy Book, and when we're in dock, a'body sees them. Even before we come in to the dock they see them. The words tell the folk what it is we're doin'."

Laughter followed these words, and Cook winked at Betsy before saying, "Aye, an' elephants can fly! How many folk in they wilds can read it?"

Hamish, offended but still anxious to explain and defend the work of *Revelation*, struggled with it. "More than you think, lass. I'm tellin' ye this. Efter Bruce showed me how to read the Bible, I wanted to tell everybody aboot Jesus. Maist o' the folk aboot the isles are the same as I was mysel', before the boat couped, and well, you baith ken that story."

Cook MacLaren produced her well-worn Bible from a shelf in the pantry. "Here's the Book. Read it to us, Betsy." As she finished reading the verse, Betsy asked: "What's a' that aboot fires, then, Hamish?"

"Och, aye, I asked Bruce aboot that when he first tellt me this. It disna mean fires like the one in the kitchen range here. It means the fire inside a body when he's thinking aboot the

Lord an' wants tae show a'body. Bruce has that kind o' fire, and he wants to smit others wi' it. They call that revival. He says the Lord would have him shout it fae the sea to the inhabitants o' the isles, and that's what he's doin'. Even preachin' fae the boat when we canna get close enough to land. There ye have it."

Betsy refilled Hamish's teacup as she asked her next question, "What do you mean about gettin' close enough to land? Are the places onything like thon picture in the parlor? Waves as big as hooses an. . . ."

Hamish smiled. He was talking a lot today, but it was nice enough. "Och, no. We stay at the farm in Aribaig when the waves would be like that. Mind, the odd storm comes up, but no, our worst troubles are the shallows, and sometimes we get pelted!"

Betsy gave a small scream. "Pelted! Like the time thon Jeremy was in the riot?"

"Oh, that wasna so bad. We've had worse nor that, but he's no' feart. He says the Lord takes care of His own when they're aboot His work." All at once Hamish got up from the table. "Talking aboot work, I better see if he needs me for onything."

"He'll ring, if he does." Betsy's words met the air as Hamish disappeared.

The cook was nodding off to sleep, and Betsy, too, wanted her bed, but she still had something on her mind. "If the Lord takes care o' his own, what aboot Miss Jean?"

But Cook MacLaren snored on.

27

At first glance the meeting hall seemed no different to Bruce. The same lady pounded her heart out on the piano, and there was the very same tambourine player, with a few more gray hairs, perhaps, but then who hadn't? Glancing upward, he realized that a new ceiling covered the place where water stains had patterned it. Another look confirmed, too, that the piano was new. Mr. Bennett had done that, no doubt. The rules here had their own fastnesses. The richer members were politely asked not to donate more than their tithe, and missionaries were diligently supported before any money was spent on the home building.

Suddenly Bruce's gaze, sweeping the hall for changes, caught a stranger at the back—a stranger yet somehow familiar. Could it be? Yes, it was! The famous reformer from London Town, Charles Booth himself. Bruce felt a sinking inside that he had not experienced for many years. What was that atheist doing here? Immediately he was reprimanded within his spirit. This was the house of the Lord, and all who entered were welcomed without question. His name was being called, and Bruce rose to give his address.

". . . So I'm not here to talk about the difficulties facing our world and our land. Those problems are too great for me. I'll just try to bring things into perspective and to the level of one person at a time." During the reading from the Bible, Bruce had not allowed himself to look again at the occupants of the back row. His text was from the Gospel of John and concerned the story of Nicodemus.

"Jesus gave the answer for all when he told Nicodemus. 'Ye must be born again'! Visualize this great man, Nicodemus—a ruler of the Jews, a professor of religion, filled with Jewish culture, customs, politics. See him sputtering and gesticulating 'What? You must be jesting! How can a grown man go back into the womb and be born again?' or words similar to that. Patiently Jesus tells him, 'No, not that. It is a spiritual rebirth I am speaking of. The water to cleanse, the blood to bring new life, and the Holy Spirit to quicken into action by His power, that's what it means to be born again!' There is not much more about Nicodemus in the New Testament, but the small mention after the resurrection proves he must have done it. He came to ask, and he received an answer. It describes a new start, a new beginning." Bruce paused for breath.

Not a sound broke the stillness as he went on, "Do you ever dream of being washed clean from every bad thing that's ever happened to you? There is nothing you have done that is too bad for Jesus to forgive, if you repent. He will give you a fresh start and a completely clean slate. You can be like Nicodemus, who hid in the background until it was almost too late, or you can step up now and join the ranks of the redeemed. 'Be born again.' Just say, 'Jesus, I want this to happen to me. Help me to have it. I want the water to cleanse me of my past, all of it, and I want the blood to give me new life. Then I want the Holy Spirit to quicken me to action.'

"Jesus Christ Himself has to be the answer to our world's problems. He was in Nicodemus's day, He is now, and He always will be the only hope for a world that God loves so much He sent His only Son in person to save it. Stop wondering if it might work, and try it! You won't know until you do. What have you got to lose? As the miracle of that new birth starts to work in you from the inside out, and as it happens simultaneously to others the world over, true Christianity will break forth from the merger. The kind you've longed for and wondered about. Stop looking to others to make it work, only you and I can make it work!"

The silence lingered for moments before a shout of "Amen, brother" gave the signal for all to join in. A dozen or more people came to the front, and the deacon-board members, including Bruce's friend Benny, went to speak with the newcomers.

George whispered to Bruce, "You saw him, didn't you?"

"Yes, I saw him, but my address has been simmering in my mind for a week or more, so it had to be the Lord's Word for him. Did he respond?"

"He ran out the moment you finished, but the Lord is dealing with him, I know. He's more the type to confess in private."

"The Word says we must confess Him before men!"

"I know, and he will, maybe not for a while, but he will. The hound of heaven is after him!"

No one was surprised when George returned to his home that night to find a note from Charles Booth, stating he had been called to London on an urgent matter. George smiled as he prayed. "Make him Yours, Lord. He's running, but he's nearly ready."

Next day the postman left a surprising letter at Strathcona House. It was from Beulah's daughter and, of course, Jean's mother, Jessica Irvine. Jessica simply informed her mother that Cameron had at last succumbed to the climate of his beloved Punjab, and she, Jessica, would be coming home a widow, maybe even arriving at the same time as the post. She would be bringing her Indian maid, Larissa, but Raju and Faye Felicity would be staying at the mission in Calcutta for one more year.

A careful scan of the envelope and Beulah was able to conclude that indeed the group should, and likely would, arrive within a few more days. Bruce decided to await his mother-in-law's arrival, but immediately after greeting her, he would take his family back to Aribaig. This summer he would do something different and take the boat even further north, maybe round John o' Groat's. An extra week would give them a grand start.

"Mary Jean MacAlister is the most blessed wee lassie I know. She's got two great-grannies, two grannies, two great-gran'pas, one gran'pa, and she has more aunties and uncles and cousins than I can count."

"Whoa there, Jeremy, you're making my head spin, just trying to keep up with you. You're wrong about aunties and uncles. Except for Hamish, she would have no other uncles. Her mother was an only child, and so is Reverend Bruce. Hamish is Bruce's stepbrother and no blood relation at all!" Elspeth was out of breath by the time she finished this genealogy, and now she said, "Catch the other end of that tick, while I ease it from this side."

Jeremy obediently caught the immense feather tick and waited for further directions.

"I want it out the window, seeing we put that pile of old sheets under there to catch it."

"I see, you want me to shove it out the window? The now, you mean?"

"Yes, Jeremy, the now!" The annual spring cleaning was well advanced at the Mains. Roddy MacDonald was whitewashing the outside walls, while Jeremy helped Elspeth with the heavier inside jobs.

"Look out below!" he yelled now as they manipulated the awkward burden through the narrow opening. It was Bruce's old attic room, but Jeremy had no trouble with bumping his head on the coomb ceiling, as he had hardly grown in the four years since the Cormacks had taken him into their home.

He may not have grown in stature, but in every other way his maturity never ceased to amaze Elspeth. Now she laughed as she asked him, "Where did you hear the saying, 'Look out below,' Jeremy?"

"Hamish! When he told me thon stories about when he was a sailor that time."

"Oh, you must not believe all Hamish's stories, Jeremy. He exaggerates, you know. Get up on that box now, and I'll hand you the pail of distemper. Are you sure you want your room painted blue?"

"I'm sure." Elspeth turned to make her way down the stairs, but the sixteen-year-old's next words stopped her. "Mistress, you know, I *do* believe Hamish, after he told me about the Lord Jesus not being pleased if we give false witness. That's telling lies, isn't it?"

"Yes, it is. I'm sorry, Jeremy, but I'm still not used to Hamish being a new person, even after all this time."

"I know. That year I went to school in Aribaig, Hamish warned me that folk who knew him before would laugh at him being converted and that they wouldn't trust me either at first—maybe never."

Jeremy's rhythmic strokes with the brush faltered only slightly as he recalled the battles he had dodged in those early days—not just because he was to turn the other cheek, but because the fellows were too big and too many for him to handle alone. Only once had he stood up, and that was when a bully called Reverend MacAlister a liar. Jeremy came home from school that day battered and bleeding but triumphant, along with his friend Aloysius MacLeod—Al for short—whose daddy was the policeman.

Jeremy turned round to smile at Elspeth. The smile transformed the small face, and Elspeth's heart went out to the boy. He liked talking about family relationships, because he had never experienced any of the real kind. Her next job could wait a few more minutes.

"So if Mary Jean has only one uncle, what about Dr. Peter and his wife and the twins? What about Miss Faye Felicity, in India, and Miss Amelia and Mr. Bennett and—"

"All friends of Bruce's and Jean's. The titles *auntie* and *uncle* are what they call courtesy titles."

Jeremy absorbed this for a while. "I'm always learnin' more things, and I like that. Reverend Bruce likes it, too, doesn't he?"

"He does indeed. Jeremy, have you thought of going somewhere else to learn more and different things?" The brush ceased abruptly and a look of genuine astonishment, with a hint of fear, confronted Elspeth.

"What for, mistress? Everything I want the now is here at Mains. I'm learnin' from Gran'pa Bruce an' you an' Maister Andrew. Yesterday I helped wi' the sheep, gettin' them ready for the shearin', an' I'm gettin' good at the milkin', am I not? Like maister says, somebody has to put the porridge an' ham an' eggs on Scotland's breakfast tables."

Ashamed, Elspeth could hardly meet the frank stare. She reached up and touched him briefly, almost overcome with compassion for the boy. "I'll away downstairs and get the tea ready. The other men will be in soon. Dugald will be here any minute with the post, and this is the day he starts to train his replacement, so that'll be one extra."

All at once she recalled the feather mattress, and she wailed, "Oh, Jeremy, with all this talk, I forgot to put the tick on the dike to air. Come on, I'll need you to help me to lift it." Pulling off her cap, she ran her fingers through almost completely white hair. At fifty-two years old, Elspeth Cormack was not unaware of how attractive she looked as she ran downstairs. In actual fact she felt younger than she had ten years ago, when Bruce had first left for the university. She had finally, in the past few years, begun to take seriously her husband's admonition to "be anxious for nothing!" and Gran'pa Bruce's "let go and let God take care of it."

28

Dugald's replacement tried to hide his bewilderment. The way the old fellow raved on about this family, you'd think his whole job was to bring the post over the bridge and hence to the Mains Farm and never mind the rest of the crofts and farms and cottages on the route. The bicycles were safely propped up against the lonely rowan tree while the two official representatives of her majesty's royal mail marched across the steading. A frantic dog met them, and it seemed its name was *Melancholy*. Apparently old Dugald, walking beside him, thought the name to be the funniest joke. The dog was more than nine years old, but it ran to meet them like a two-year-old. What was this coming now? It looked for all the world like a feather tick with two pairs of legs. Even Dugald halted at that sight, mouth wide open and eyes staring, before he recognized the legs barely visible under the folds of the mattress.

"It's a' richt, Taylor, yon's the mistress carryin' the tick, and by the looks of it, the young lad I was tellin' ye aboot is helpin' her. He's the one Constable Neal—"

"Aye, Dugald, I mind it fine. It maun be spring-cleanin' time again. My mither goes daft then, too, wi' a' thing washed and scoured and hung on the line, 'til the life is battered oot of it. Then ye hardly ken the place efter."

"That's a fact a'thegither! I'm glad I've nay wumman to do yon to ma hoose." He returned to his favorite subject: "Reverend Bruce is no' here the now, but the letters in yer bag will gie us all the latest doin's of himself and Hamish and Mary Jean." They had arrived on the doorstep, and a flushed Elspeth, with Jeremy close behind, met them there.

"Come away in, Dugald. The kettle's on the boil, and the scones are today's baking."

"Aye, thank ye, Mistress Cormack. This is Taylor Ferguson; he'll be takin' ower my route." The kitchen suddenly seemed full of men, and Taylor quietly waited until all the greetings ended.

A man he knew to be Andrew Cormack addressed him, "Taylor Ferguson, ye're not from Aribaig, then?"

"No, I'm from Mallaig." Taylor would have said no more, but Andrew was determined to draw him into the conversation. By now the group sat around the enormous kitchen table. That the new postman was shocked at the familiarity displayed by Dugald, who was a terrible show-off with a newcomer, Andrew knew. Shocked or not, he still ate his fill of the scones, spread thick with the golden butter and jam Elspeth had piled on the table, and washed the lot down with copious amounts of tea.

"Are ye a family man then, Taylor?"

Taylor turned crimson, but he was not displeased at the question. "Not yet, Mr. Cormack, but I'm gettin' married on Saturday."

"Is that a fact? You'll be off for a day or two, then?"

"Oh, no, this is my first job as a postman. I'll be out on Monday with the letters."

"Is your wife-to-be from Mallaig as well?"

"She's not, Jessie's fae Aribaig and goes to yer ain kirk, Mr. Cormack. I saw you there on Sunday."

"Oh, I see. Yes, I heard the banns but didn't put the names together till the now. Wee Jessie Cowan, is it?"

"Aye, Jessie Cowan." Saying the name seemed to render him speechless, and Taylor subsided again.

Andrew pressed on. "Jessie Cowan, she comes to the 'New Life' Bible class, does she not?"

"She does that. She got converted at a meeting with Reverend MacAlister, in Aribaig, about four year ago. She tellt me all aboot it an' aboot the reverend gettin' pelted by the crowd."

"You don't approve, Taylor?"

The younger man was obviously flustered. Too polite to speak up or say anything that might reflect on his host's family, yet he was that naive being—a truly honest man. "Beggin' your pardon, Mr. Cormack, but you're right, I don't a'thegither approve of yon clappin' an' shoutin'. After all 'What doth the Lord require of thee, but—' "

" '. . . To do justly, and to love mercy, and to walk humbly with thy God?' " It was Elspeth who finished the verse.

The others in the room had been listening for a while, without Taylor realizing it. He blushed again as Gran'pa spoke, "Micah six, verse eight You're well acquainted with the Scriptures, then, Taylor?"

"Aye. Is it no time to go now then, Dugald?" But it was another half hour before they left, and by that time Taylor had invited the whole family to his wedding on Saturday. His news that Reverend Fraser Clegg, on leave from the missionary society, would be performing the ceremony set up another spate of memories. Fraser had married the bride's parents, twenty years earlier. In the end it was Dugald who had to drag Taylor off to their waiting bicycles.

Roddy and Jeremy returned to their brush wielding. Elspeth sat on with Andrew and Gran'pa to discuss the news from Bruce: the meeting in George Bennett's church, which Charles Booth attended; Dr. Peter Blair and his family's latest doings; Beulah and her daughter, who seemed to be forming a better relationship since the latter became a widow; and last but not least, to Elspeth, the chance encounter with Dr. Alexander. The professor had invited Bruce to his private rooms, and the two had talked for a good hour.

The letter ended: "I am giving much serious thought and prayer to his suggestions. We'll be home by Friday Your son and grandson, Bruce MacAlister."

The anxious expression appeared briefly on Elspeth's face, and the two men, who knew every line and nuance, waited.

"Whatever it is will be his decision, and the Lord will guide. I got a letter from my mother! Father is speaking a few syllables. She says he is responding to her reading from the Bible. Oh, Andrew, do you think—?"

"It could be, Elspeth, lass, nothing is too hard for our God, and He knows we've been praying hard enough. Do you want to go to Edinburgh, then?"

"Och, no, I've too much to see to here and they'll all be home on Friday. I'll wait until they leave on the *Revelation*, then we'll see." Pleased with her, the others returned to their work, but Elspeth sat on, recalling the words quoted by the new postman. "What doth the Lord require of thee . . . ?" So long had that been her own theme when she thought Bruce overexuberant about certain aspects of his ministry. She remembered the last time she had said it to him as if it were yesterday and not the occasion of his first embarking on the sea-isles crusade. Reluctantly she had gone with them on that first "tour of inspection" as the men had called it. She had been in the tiny cabin with Bruce and Mary Jean. Andrew and Gran'pa Bruce had gone with Hamish for some last-minute supplies.

She had murmured the verse, but her son had heard, and it was his reply she would never forget: "Mother, I know what you think, and I know you mean well, but what that Scripture verse says is only a starting point. For some it ends there, and that's all right for them. For others it goes further—a lot further. As for me, my call is to go as far as I can for as long as I am able. If Saint Paul had stopped at the passive state of merely being for the Lord, his soul would have been fine eternally, but then how much longer would the rest of the world, including Scotland, have had to wait for someone else to hear the call and obey it? The same applies to Saint Columba and many others, too. I believe there is much we do not know of the ones who heard and answered the call but who did not gain fame. I pray I will be allowed to meet them all someday."

"But son, what about the kirk? You have such a gift and. . . ." The yearning in her heart could not be hidden.

"Yes, Mam, the kirk. Well! I'll admit they need something or somebody, but I'm not so sure it's me, so for the now I'm still ordained but without a parish. In that state I could remain for a while yet."

"Will you?"

"I said for the now. Could we leave it at that, Mother?"

And she had left it at that. Until today. The letter said he was praying about it, and that could mean. . . . Oh, she was afraid to hope, well, no, maybe not *afraid* exactly, but not quite daring, either.

29

The first flurry of arrival was over, and at last Elspeth had her son to herself. Between them they had exhausted all the news of family and friends, and now the subject nearest Elspeth's own heart could be kept in no longer.

"Can you not tell me what Dr. Alexander had to say, Bruce?"

"I've been thinking of that, Mam, but I'm still not sure how I want to answer him. He told me there's been some changes in the kirk's administration and some of the rulings. Anyway, to make his long-winded treatise short, he suggested I consider being reinstated, and he even had an offer of a living for me, if I decided to accept."

"Oh, Bruce, what did you say to that?"

"As I've just told you, Mam, I haven't decided at all yet." He gazed round the familiar room, his thoughts off someplace where she could not follow. Elspeth waited. At last she had learned something about waiting. He would tell her in his own way and time. Maybe not today but. . . . His voice broke through her musings, and she started.

"I've enjoyed the freedom of the boat ministry: the waking to the gulls cry and watching the sunrise over the water or the land, depending on where we are; the excitement of setting up the meetings with Hamish and others among the men who love the Lord, from time to time; the thrill of standing up in the boat when the people throng the shore to listen. Jesus had to do that, too, remember, when they had no other meeting place. And Mam, yon isle away up in Wester Ross, where the folk still worshiped the standin' stones, and after we'd stayed there a fortnight, the whole population of the island got converted." Bruce's eyes grew misty as he thought of the Lord's triumph and the angels' rejoicing on that day.

His mother sat, hardly daring to breathe, as he continued, "I've been praying much, and I hope I practice enough of my own preaching to realize that because a body enjoys doing something doesn't mean that it's sinful!" They exchanged smiles.

"All the same there is starting in my spirit an uneasiness. My thoughts go out to ones like Grandfather Munro. For fifty years or more he was a 'staunch pillar' of yon big church in Morningside, while inside him a brood of vipers ate away at his own soul and his body as well. Doctors are proving this kind of thing to be true. In many cases, ulcers and other grave ills come from the hidden man—we would say the hidden sins of man. There are thousands like that, Mam, who need to be shown that God is not a hard, cruel taskmaster, who hates them, but is loving and kind and just." He paused once more, this time leaning over to touch her hands, folded idly in her lap.

"Leaving all that for the now, then, Mam, this offer from Dr. Angry—at first I said no outright, when he told me one reason they wanted me was because I do seem to attract the crowds, but after that the unease started. Always before, when I've had a big decision, the answer would settle in my heart, and I'd be sure. This time I'm dithering from one side to the other like the boat at anchor before we set the sails for it to go north or south, east or west."

At last Elspeth felt free to speak. "Son, I've had my struggles, too, with selfish reasons for what you should do, but here is what I'm thinking this minute. You've come to a place of maturity in God, and now He wants you to decide for yourself. Oh, I know you must pray, and you have; you must obey direct guidance, and you have. Choosing between good and evil for the likes of you is simple. Choosing between two goods, it's not so simple. I can say all this to you, but you know yourself that the last deciding factor is up to you." Bruce gazed at his mother with fresh insight. This was a different Elspeth, the Edinburgh lawyer plus something else he couldn't quite define, and she was right.

Loud shrieks interrupted them as a small body catapulted into the kitchen and onto Elspeth's lap.

"The tigers are coming, Gran'speth!" The voice didn't sound too frightened, and seconds later Melancholy and Jeremy followed at a rush. A bevy of puppies came next, yapping and yipping. Elspeth didn't even scold. She was too happy. Everything necessary to this point had been said. Pretending outrage, she rose and chased the jungle safari out of her kitchen.

An unbroken landscape faced them in a chain of high rugged peaks, and Hamish, busy with the rigging, called out to Bruce. "Nae openin' here and so nae use tryin' to anchor. Should we no' pull round an' let the breeze tack us to the next isle? I dinna' think any folk bide here."

"I'll admit it seems like that, but I feel there's folk on the other side of these formidable, timeless rocks." Hamish sighed. When Bruce talked in big words like that it meant he was communing and wouldn't be making much sense for a while.

An hour later, as they rounded a headland, Bruce spotted the narrow sea lane leading into a natural harbor. He knew he was a clumsy deckhand, but Hamish's skill made up for his lack, so between them they managed. Maneuvering the small craft to where she could ride at anchor proved fairly simple.

Bruce wiped his brow. "I often think of the goodness of the Lord in providing you with the skills of navigation, Hamish. I'm sure I would have floundered on rocks like these many times but for you."

"Och, man, if it hadna' been me, it would have been another, maybe a better sailor. I wouldna' call it yon fancy name, either. Chust a way of makin' a livin' I learnt after leavin' the croft."

"Whatever way it happened, I'm glad you're here with us."

Hamish leaped ashore, and after securing the line to a rough stone pillar nearby, he proceeded to haul the craft alongside the primitive jetty. Bruce's feelings had been right, he thought, as he caught a glimpse of other boats, hidden in the shallows. As no other signs of life appeared, they continued the routine of docking and setting up, which was now reduced to a fine art after four years of working it out together.

Soon the welcome fragrance of bacon frying wafted from the tiny galley, bringing a lively shout from below decks. "Uncle Hamie! . . . Daddy!"

For their earlier journeys Hamish had secured the cabin for Mary Jean's safety by the simple method of erecting a combination cage and bed for her. In it she could play or sleep in safety. Past that stage now, she still needed help to get out of it.

About the only flaw in the otherwise idyllic life-style surrounding Mary Jean MacAlister could be that her every wish became law as long as it wasn't known to be harmful. Plenty of willing slaves awaited her in whichever environment she found herself, and she knew of nothing else.

Once only had Bruce spanked his daughter. Hamish had gone ashore for supplies that day, and she had slipped away from her father's side and started up the rigging. Like a little cat, she had kept out of his reach. Again like a cat, she could move no further for sudden fear. When he had at last grasped her and lowered her down safely to the deck, his own fear had materialized in a scolding and a sharp smack on the bottom.

Later he held her close and explained. She gazed up at him, large eyes shining with unshed tears.

"Mary Jean, do you like being here on the boat with your uncle and me?" They always conversed as two adults.

"Aye?" Her brogue, with its mixture of tongues from all those with whom she spent her days, sounded clear through her wondering.

"Should you have an accident and be hurt, we could not be bringing you on our journeys round the isles anymore!" Big tears now flooded the velvet eyes, and Bruce had to concentrate his own gaze upward for a moment before he could continue in his resolve. "Then your grannies would be after me. Granny Cormack would say, 'I told you a boat was no place for a wee lass!' Now if you ever do that again, and you know what I'm meaning, I'd have to agree with them. What do you think would happen then, Mary Jean?"

"I'd have to stay at Mains or Granny Mac's myself." The last word choked out, and Bruce again avoided looking directly at the diminutive face.

The sentence told it all. For half the year their time was divided between Glasgow and Aribaig, with short day trips to Morningside in the spring and autumn. Mary Jean was a happy little girl who enjoyed all the aspects of her life, without knowing or caring how different that life was from other children's. She visited the noisy Blair house when they went to Glasgow, and she liked everybody there, but she always liked going home again. Mary Jean loved all her grannies and the menfolk who bowed to her wishes, but her daddy was her best love. When he left her anywhere, even for just an hour or two, she retreated into a silent world of her own. So when she choked on the word *myself*, Bruce knew that she had learned her lesson and he had said enough.

After that, the tether came back into use. This was a type of harness, also one of Hamish's inventions, which he strapped across her shoulders and attached to the main mast.

One day Hamish announced, "She's too big for that thing." Gladly it was dispensed with.

Today, as Bruce made his way down the short stairway, Hamish called, "She doesna' need to be snecked in any mair. I'll dismantle that thing."

Ablutions and toilet arrangements, primitive but effective, were another cause of conflict with both his mother and Granny Mac. Bruce agreed that these could be better and would say no more. Within himself he knew it was one of the penalties he must pay for the pearl of great price of keeping his daughter with him as he went about his ministry. Bringing an extra person aboard, and a female at that, to help care for the child, was unthinkable.

All these thoughts and memories flashed quickly through Bruce's mind as he and Mary Jean came back to the galley. His talk with Elspeth was causing him to have many deeply introspective thoughts. He knew it was indeed time to consider Dr. Alexander's proposal. However, he had until August to think about it, so he determined to enjoy the summer. He had no doubts that the right decision would come at the right time. His task for today was to discover if any souls lived on this isle, and if so, would they want what he had to offer?

30

Only his mother knew how this summer's journey round the isles might be the final one for the Reverend Bruce MacAlister. His letters arrived at Mains farm irregularly, depending on where he found a posting place. Some isles had one, some only a weekly or monthly boat, while some lonely islanders asked him to post their letters.

Taylor, now well initiated in his job as postman, but forever to be dubbed the "New Postie," had one such letter in his bag today. He had other letters, too, though he did not follow Dugald's example of detection, but allowed the recipients to find out for themselves where their letters came from.

Gran'pa sliced open the fat missive and read out the doings as usual. Elspeth listened politely during the readings, but her thoughts rested in a smaller envelope, tucked in her apron pocket at this moment, waiting for the time when she would be alone. At last the kitchen was empty, and she held the sealed note up to the light.

She smiled at memories of Dugald doing just this and Andrew saying, "Thon envelope's told you all it will without somebody opening it." Finally she took up the letter opener that had replaced the old gully knife. Bruce had brought it back from one of his trips to the far northern isles. A cairngorm handle, set in the blunt blade, was inscribed with the first line of the Shepherd Psalm. Elspeth whispered the words to herself now as she wielded the small tool.

Unfolding the sheet of paper, her wayward thoughts now quoting Shakespeare's "To be or not to be," she read the single line of print: *"It's to be the kirk!"*

Calling to Jeremy to leave the job and fetch the men, Elspeth reached into the cupboard under the stairs and brought out an instrument she had never thought to use before. Pulling off her apron and cap, she skipped to the door. A glorious sun beat down on her wonderful world, even more wonderful since a few minutes ago. Startled, Andrew came running, followed more slowly by Gran'pa Bruce. With mouths agape, they watched the sedate Elspeth Munro MacAlister Cormack dance out into the middle of the steading, feet bare and skirts kilted, waving a tambourine. Behind her pranced Jeremy and Roddy and the troop of dogs. She was pouring her heart out in song.

"I will sing unto the Lord for He has triumphed gloriously, the horse and rider thrown into the sea. I will sing unto the Lord for he has triumphed gloriously and this is the will of God concerning thee!"